Forever Mine

Whiskey Men 4

Hope Ford

Chapter 1

Natalie

I'm surrounded by the heat from Beau's body, and I want to burrow deeper into him, but I don't dare. I hope that he stays in bed a little longer. My leg is over his, and my arm is over his chest, while my face is buried into his neck. It's like I've completely wrapped myself around him sometime in the night, and now I don't want to move.

It's in our bedroom where he's most open to any kind of intimacy. If I start to move or shift in any way, he'll find a reason to get out of bed and start his day.

So I lie here quietly, taking small breaths, making no sudden movements, and relishing the feel of him next to me.

I'm just hoping to get a few minutes of feeling his body next to mine. This is when I feel the closest to him. This is one of the reasons that I stay. It's this side of him, behind closed doors when it's just the two of us, that I feel loved by my husband. Any other time, I feel like I'm a roommate or even worse, sometimes a nuisance.

I take a deep breath, inhaling the woodsy scent of his aftershave that he put on after his shower last night. I try to commit everything to memory. The way he feels, the soft noises he makes in his sleep, the feel of his stubble against my cheek.

Can I really give this up? Later today, when I'm wide awake and am looking at the full picture, I know I will need to leave him. It's time. Hell, it's way past time. But when we're like this and with his hand on my back, holding me to him like he can't let me go, like he doesn't want to let me go, well, I'm not so sure my plan to leave is the right thing to do.

I know the instant he wakes up because his body becomes tense, and he seems to hold his breath. I'm not ready for this to end. I need one last time with him, even though I know it's shitty. I know it makes me an ass to ask him to make love to me when I know

I'm asking him for a divorce later today, but I need to feel his love one more time. I need to get lost in his touch so I can carry it with me.

I slide my hand down his chest, past his belly and to the waistband of his underwear. Goosebumps rise on his arms, and when I dip my hand into his shorts, he grunts out my name. "Nat... argh."

I smile against his neck and kiss him until he sucks in a breath and grips me tighter. If this is going to be our last time together, I want to make it good.

I kiss across his shoulder and down his chest. Going to my knees, I pull at his shorts, and he lifts his hips so I can pull them down. I kiss his navel, pressing my tongue to his hot skin before going down. I move over him until I'm sitting on my knees between his legs, and for the first time, I look into his eyes. "Morning," I tell him with my sleep-laden voice.

He smiles at me. "And what a good morning, too."

I look at the clock on the nightstand and take note that he has awhile before he has to leave for work. "You need to rush out of here?"

His head falls back, and he moans as my hands roam over his abdomen. "No. I got time... I'll make time."

I press my lips to him, savoring the taste of his skin.

My emotions surge, but I don't relent. The early light is glaring through the curtains, and my body is on full display. Any other time, I'd be self-conscious, but knowing this will most likely be our last time together, I don't let myself feel any insecurities. I refuse to. Instead, I try to get lost in the moment and the way he makes me feel.

I need more, and I need it all. But at the same time, I don't want to rush things.

Beau reaches down between us and pulls at my lace panties. His thumb trails back and forth across my lower belly, causing me to suck in a gulp of air. "You like these panties?"

I shrug, gyrating my hips slowly across his belly. "Yes. Do you like them?"

He grunts his answer. "Yeah, but I would like them better off."

I am about to lift up to take them off when both his hands grip my hips to hold me in place. "No, I got it."

He grabs the lace in his hands and with a steady pull, he rips the string of my panties on first my right side and then my left. He grabs the shreds of material and tosses them on the floor. He reaches for the nightstand, and it takes everything in me to hold back. I want to tell him I'm on the pill, but he already knows that. I want to tell him that just once, I want to feel him bare, but it's nothing that he hasn't heard from me before. He doesn't want children, and I didn't find that out until after our wedding. But I did discover the lengths he'd go to make sure we don't have any. He will do whatever's necessary, even wearing a condom every time we're together since my birth control isn't one hundred percent effective.

He grabs the condom from the drawer and rips the wrapper, and I move back so that he can sheathe himself.

He flips me over until he's hovering over top of me. He leans down and kisses my lips, down my throat and across my chest.

He takes a deep breath, gritting his teeth. He's always been a man of restraint. He demands control in every situation. I slide my hands up his chest and hook them around his neck.

I should take what he's willing to give me but even now, knowing this could be my last day with him, I'm going to challenge him. "You don't always have to be in control, you know. You can do what you want to with me, Beau. Whatever you want, I'll like it."

He clenches his eyes shut tight and shakes his head. His whole body seems to swell over me, and a vein in his neck is vibrating. I squeeze his shoulders, wanting him to unleash, but he doesn't. He pries his eyes open and stares down at me. "Damn, you're so beautiful."

My eyes widen in surprise, and all I can do is murmur, "Thank you."

With a grunt, he asks, "What do you need, Nat? Because you feel so fucking good, I'm not going to last."

I grab his hand and move it to my hip. "This. I need your hands on me, Beau. That's it."

He doesn't disappoint. I'm ready, and I've been thinking about this for hours before he woke up. Before long, we're both completely engulfed in a mutual earth-shattering, body-trembling climax. He grunts as he collapses on top of me. We're both breathing heavily, and he's holding his weight off me, but I wrap my legs around his waist, trying to pull him to me. I'm completely satisfied, but I'm not ready to let go.

He kisses my cheek. "I need to get up and get ready for work."

When I don't answer him, he tries to lift me off, but I stop him by holding my legs around him tighter.

He rears back to look at me with a small smirk on his face. "Nat? I need to get ready."

There are a thousand things I want to say to him, but I know it's not the time or the place. I'll have to do that later. I'm not going to ruin this moment of what will possibly be our last time together, so I unlatch my legs from around him.

He climbs off the bed and walks straight into the bathroom without a second glance my way. "I love you," I mutter into the empty room.

Chapter 2

Natalie

I stare at my phone, my finger hovering over the send button.

I typed out the four words, and this is the hardest text I've ever prepared to send. The longer I stare at the words on the phone, the more uneasy I get.

I know I just need to do it. I need to hit send and then deal with the consequences, but I can't seem to make myself do it. I delete the text and then lay the phone down on the table in front of me.

I push myself away from the table and stand up. I need to think about it some more. At least consider my options. It's a big decision, and it shouldn't be made lightly.

I pace the length of the dining room. There are eight chairs surrounding the huge custom-made table. The hutch at the other end of the room is filled with expensive china, and the chandelier is worth more than both my parents make in a year. But it's all too much, and I'm feeling claustrophobic.

I grab my phone off the table and my sweater off the back of the chair and make my way to the sliding doors that lead to the back yard.

As soon as I walk out into the open air, I take a deep breath and sit down on the chaise lounge. I watch as the lights surrounding the pool dance off the reflection of the water. There's a light on at the pool house, but other than that, darkness surrounds me.

I think back through the last two years and wonder how I got it so wrong. I grew up with two parents completely in love. We didn't have much, but our family never lacked love. I always hoped I would find a love like the one my parents have, and I thought I'd found it with Beau. I'm not sure what I did wrong. My stomach knots up just thinking about what I'm about to do.

I lean my head back and look up at the starry sky and get lost in thought. Beau was everything from the first moment I saw him. He would come into the diner I worked at in Jasper, and I knew immediately he was someone special. He came in every day, flirted with me, and left me big tips. I was completely won over by him and looking for him to come in every night. I thought it was innocent enough until he asked me out, and only then did I begin to hope that there could be something between us.

He was always guarded with his heart, but he showered me with gifts, and it was all a little overwhelming. Growing up, there was never any extra money. It never really bothered me until I was in high school. It was then my friends were getting cars when they turned 16 or brand-new dresses for prom or were able to go on fancy vacations while I stayed home in the summer and worked.

I met Beau when I was only 24, and when he spent money on me like it was no big deal, I felt loved. Even though now I realize that's not what it was. It's never been about love for Beau. At least on his side. For me, I fell hard and I fell fast. I saw the man behind the money, and even though I told him he didn't have to spend money on me, he did anyway.

And when he asked me to marry him, I said yes. I knew our relationship wasn't perfect, but I was so in love there's no way I would have considered saying no. I wanted to be Mrs. Beau Blaze more than anything, and even if sometimes I wondered if he truly loved me, I thought he wouldn't have asked me if he didn't. So I told him yes, and we planned out the most beautiful wedding Whiskey Run had ever seen.

And now, only two years later, I know that I was wrong. Does Beau care about me? Yes, he does. Does he love me? No, he doesn't. At this point, I'm pretty sure he doesn't need me either. We live completely separate lives, and the only time there is any intimacy between us is at night behind closed doors. And when that happens, I think that things are going to be different. He's going to let his guard down and open his heart.

But the very next minute, when he refuses to cuddle or even hold me afterwards, I know that nothing has changed.

And I hate myself for it.

I thought it was enough and that I could keep going like we were.

I've settled for a marriage with hardly any intimacy, taking what I can get from him. Any amount of time he'll give me, I've taken it. He bought me the gym I own downtown where I teach. He makes sure that I drive a new car. I have new clothes and jewelry and can do whatever I want to. He's made it that I want for nothing, at least material-wise... but it's not enough.

Because the truth is, I want more. I deserve more, and I'm not going to settle for anything less. Not anymore.

Everything he gives me is nice, but I can do without all of it because the only thing I truly want he can't give me.

He has his heart guarded, and after two years of marriage, he hasn't wavered at all. He's held me at arm's length, and no matter how hard I try or how much I want it, I can't get any closer.

I open the messaging app on my phone. It's ridiculous to text him knowing he's right inside, but this is the best way to get his attention. I could walk into his home office, but he wouldn't even lift his head to look at me. He'd be completely focused on the computer screen in front of him, and I'd feel like I'm an intruder in my own home.

No, this is the way I need to do it. He may read it tonight or not until tomorrow, but I know I need to get it out. I type the words, taking a breath between each one. *I want a divorce.*

I stare at the black letters and try to imagine my life without Beau. It's not any kind of life I want, but I need to do this.

I hit send and wait for relief, grief, or whatever it is to hit me. For just a minute, I panic. My heart races, I feel heat rush through my body, and I second-guess myself, but just as quickly, the feeling disappears, and in its place comes acceptance. I had to do this. I had to. Deep down, I know that I won't be truly happy going on the way we are.

I lay the phone in my lap and lean my head back. Instead of looking up at the stars, I close my eyes and try to think about what I need to do next. And maybe there's just a small part of me that hopes my husband is going to fight for me... for us.

Chapter 3

Beau

My phone buzzes, and instead of looking at it, I take my glasses off and rub my eyes. I worked all day at the office, came home and had dinner with Nat, and then excused myself to my office at the house. I'm caught up with the day, but there's always something that I need to read or stay on top of. Maybe Nat and I could watch a television show tonight. We haven't done that in a while.

My phone dings again with the two-minute reminder that I had a text.

I let out a sigh, put my glasses back on, grab my phone, and see there's a text from Natalie. I smile instantly, because this is how she gets my attention sometimes. Maybe she wants to watch a movie too. Heck, maybe she wants a replay from this morning.

I open the message, and my whole world shifts. I stand up but instantly get a little woozy. With my hands on the desk in front of me, I lean over, and my eyes never leave the four words that Natalie sent me. *I want a divorce.*

I shouldn't be surprised. I knew two years ago when she agreed to marry me that it wouldn't be forever. I knew she would eventually leave me. I had hoped she wouldn't and that maybe she'd come to love me, but that's not the case.

I try to get my bearings. I want to be mad and throw things, but that's not who I am. I'm the Blaze brother that is always in control. Well, normally anyway, not counting a few nights ago when I got drunk as hell and Ford and Huddy had to bring my ass home. Shit. I run my hands through my hair and try to pull myself together. I knew this was coming. The signs were all there. We normally spend the evenings together, but she's been more distant than usual.

Fuck, I guess I need to face the music.

I leave my phone on the desk and walk through the house. First stop is the living room. It's immaculate, not one thing out of place. It almost looks sterile with the white walls, carpet, and show pieces. I make my way to the kitchen, and it's empty too. I think about earlier when Nat and I worked side by side to clean up the dirty dishes from dinner. There was no big indication that the night would end with her asking for a divorce.

I make my way back to the middle of the house about to go upstairs, and that's when I notice the screen door leading outside is halfway open. There's a knot in the pit of my stomach as I make my way toward the door. Peeking out the window, I see her sitting in her favorite lounge chair with her head tilted back and her eyes closed. I stay here for just a minute, taking her in. She's beautiful. Her blond hair is spread out like a halo under her head. Without even seeing them, I can picture her blue eyes that sparkle every time she looks at me. My eyes travel down the length of her body, and instantly I'm hard. Since the day I first laid eyes on her, I've had this reaction. She's curvy, and her body is what dreams are made of. So many times I've had to hold back and not let her see how completely consumed I am by her.

Every thought I have about her has my blood racing south. What am I going to do without her? How can I let her just leave me?

I know I can't stand here all night, just stalking her.

I slide the door open the rest of the way and step through. I know the instant she knows I've joined her because her body tenses. I move to sit in the lounge chair next to her. With my feet on the ground between us, I lean forward, resting my arms on my legs. To her, I probably appear calm when in fact I'm anything but. I know my life is about to be turned upside down, and there's nothing I can do about it.

"Are we going to talk about this?"

My voice is calm, clear, and in control. None of the things I'm feeling.

She turns her head to look at me. Even in the low light, I can see the sadness on her face. "Are you even surprised, Beau?"

The way she says my name has an effect on me. Ever since the first time she said it, her voice dips in a breathy, catch your breath tone. Even now when we're talking about divorce, it does the same.

I clench my hands together. "No, I guess I can't say I am surprised. What do you want?"

She laughs and shakes her head, but the reaction doesn't match the sadness in her voice. "I should have known that you would react this way. Everything, all this, is a business transaction to you." She takes a deep breath and pulls her shoulders back. "Right, well, I would like to keep my gym. That's it. That's all I want."

I run my fingers along the stubble on my chin. There's no way that's all she wants. "First of all, the gym is yours. When I purchased it, it was put into your name immediately. There's no question about that. Second, there has to be something else you want. The house, the car, the money."

She sits up and swings her legs over the other side of the chair and stands up, then turns to face me. She locks her hands together in front of her. "If I can use the car for a while, that would be great. At least until I can get something else. But no, I don't want the money or the house. I don't want any of it."

"Damn, Nat, the car is yours. And we'll figure out some kind of alimony."

She reaches up and wipes a tear from under her eye. In all this time, I've never seen Nat cry, and I'm not sure what to make of it. She crosses her arms over her chest. "I don't want your money, Beau."

Speechless, I stare up at her. "You don't want my money? Do you know how insane that sounds, Nat? You're married to a millionaire. We've been married for two years. You have rights to a portion—"

She cuts me off. "My gym and maybe my car, that's it. I don't want anything else."

I can't stop the surprise on my face. I don't understand this, and I don't know what to say. I knew the time would come when she'd leave me, but I thought for sure she'd at least want something. But as soon as the thought comes, I want to kick myself. I don't know why I'm so confused. The truth is, over the last two years, I've had to force gifts on her. She hasn't wanted any of it. Hell, she never asked for anything. She lets her arms fall to her sides and pulls her shoulders back. "Okay, well, I'm going to go pack."

She turns to go, and I jump up from my chair. "Where are you going to go?"

She doesn't turn to look at me, but she does stop. "I'm not sure. I heard that the duplex your brother's girlfriend was living in is open. I may check it out. Until then, I can stay with one of my friends from my book club."

"No!" I say as I walk around her and stop in front of her. "You can stay here."

Again, she crosses her arms over her chest. My hands fist at my sides because I want to reach for her, but I know I can't. I'm afraid if I do, I won't be able to let her go. "You stay here, and I'll move out into the pool house."

She shakes her head. "No, I'm not taking your home. I'm sure I can find something available."

I put my hands on my hips. "What the fuck, Nat? As of an hour ago, this was our house, our home. You've decided that you don't want this... you don't want me anymore, but the fact remains, you are my wife, so you'll stay here." My voice is hard as I say it again. It's like I need to make her understand that she's still my wife. "Until the divorce is final, you are my wife, and you will stay in our house."

She looks completely lost, and I don't know what to make of any of this. She doesn't seem happy with the fact she's asking for a divorce, but she's still doing it. I point to the ceiling. "I'm going to go pack and go out to the pool house."

She lets out a sob but nods her head. "Okay."

I take three steps before I turn back to her. "Is there someone else? Is that what this is about?"

For just a second, something flashes across her face. I wonder if it's guilt, but just as quickly, the look is gone, and she's shaking her head. "I have never cheated on you, Beau. I would never have done that to you."

I open my mouth and then close it. What am I going to say? Beg her to stay and give me another chance? What's the point? She's not happy with me obviously, and I'm not going to force her to stay.

"I'll be back."

I go upstairs, and my mind is going in a thousand different directions. I've had plenty of experience packing fast for all the business trips I've been on through the years, and I pack a bag with all my bathroom stuff and then with a few suits over my shoulder, I go back downstairs. I stop in my office and grab my phone and laptop. I carry it all to the back door and set it down before searching for Nat. She's sitting at the dining room table, her head in her hands.

I want to reach for her and rub her shoulders. I can tell by the way she's sitting that she's either on the verge of a migraine or she's already there.

"Do you want me to grab your medication?"

She sighs, wiping at her face before lifting her head. She looks at me through hooded eyes. Yeah, she's definitely experiencing a migraine, but she shakes her head. "No, it's okay. I'll get it. Are you sure you want to do this, Beau?"

I'm about to tell her hell no, I don't want a divorce, but she continues. "I can go out to the pool house. It's not right for me to stay here."

I hold my hand up to stop her. "It's fine. I'll go out to the pool house. If it gets bad"—I point at her head and then at myself—"call me. I don't want you in here suffering. I can draw you a bath before I go."

My offer pains her, and she sobs as she takes a breath. "No, I'll be fine." She walks off with a muttered "Lock the door on your way out."

I watch her walk up the stairs toward our bedroom, and it takes everything in me not to follow her. But the fact that she's in pain has me staying where I am. I walk room to room downstairs, turning off lights. I make sure the front door is locked, and before I go out the back door, I set the home alarm and grab all my things.

Tomorrow, if she's feeling better, I'm going to get to the bottom of this. There has to be a reason that she asked for a divorce out of the blue, and I'm going to find out what it is.

Chapter 4

Natalie

all me back or I'm coming to find you.

I read the text from Jillian, and I know she's not lying. Of all my friends, Jillian would probably call the cops to come find me if I don't call her back soon.

I'm about to call her when my phone rings. Sure enough, it's her. "Hello, Jilly."

Even though I feel like I'm hiding it well, Jilly is one of my best friends, and she knows me better than anyone. "What's wrong? What's happening? I went to your class this morning, and you had a sub teaching."

I won't even attempt to lie to her, and it's not necessarily a lie. "Migraine," I say, hoping that's answer enough.

"Oh, honey, are you okay? Can I bring you anything?"

"I'm fine now. My head actually feels a lot better."

She's quiet for just a second and then continues, "So then I'll see you at class tonight?"

Darn it. "Uh, actually, I took the whole day off. I have a sub for my night class too."

Jilly is so quiet, I almost wonder if she's hung up. "Jilly… you there?"

"What are you not telling me?"

I sigh as I peek out the back window. When I went into the garage earlier, I saw that Beau's SUV was still in the garage, which means he's still in the pool house. It's not like him to miss work. Probably in the last two years, I can count maybe three times he has. Two of them were when he got drunk with his brothers a few nights ago, and he had to recover for both those days. The third is today.

"Natalie Blaze… answer me."

I grip the phone tighter. "I told him... I told Beau I wanted a divorce."

I hear Jilly gasp in the phone, and almost immediately, her voice softens. "Oh, Nat, honey. I'm so sorry. What did he say?"

I pace back to the kitchen and pour a glass of tea. "What do you think he said? He sure didn't beg me to change my mind or even attempt to talk me out of it. I believe his first question was to ask me what I want from him."

Jilly blows out a breath. "I just don't get it. I've seen him with you and yeah, he's not all touchy-feely, but he loves you, Nat. The way he looks at you and does little things for you. There's no convincing me otherwise."

I lean against the wall and look out the window that overlooks the pool area and backyard. I'm a fool because I've spent most of the day right here, looking outside hoping to just get a glimpse of Beau. "Jilly, he wasn't even surprised when I told him I wanted a divorce. I swear it's like he's been waiting for me to do it or something. Heck, he's probably glad to get rid of me."

"Stop, Nat. Did he say anything? Did he ask you why?"

I snort and bark out a laugh. "Yeah, he asked me if there was someone else. What a joke, right?"

When she doesn't laugh with me, there's a twinge of guilt I feel, and it gets worse when she asks, "Did you tell him about Mark?"

I choke on the tea I just took a drink of and sputter, "What about him? Why the hell would I tell Beau about Mark? I'm not interested in him at all. He has nothing to do with this."

It's as if I can hear her rolling her eyes. "Nat, stop. I know you haven't cheated on Beau, but I still think that Mark is worth mentioning."

"I don't. Plus, it doesn't even matter. Beau doesn't care. He's more worried about who gets the cars and the money than what's happening between us."

She sighs into the phone, and I know she doesn't completely understand why I'm doing what I'm doing. Since I met Jilly, she's been a fan of Beau's, and she's always tried to be my voice of reason. But right now, I don't need a voice of reason. I need my friend.

"Jilly, listen to what I'm saying. It's done. I've told him I want a divorce, and he didn't even try to talk me out of it. If anything, I think he's relieved. I get to keep my car and the gym. He moved into the pool house, and I need to find a place to live because as soon as the divorce is final, I'll be moving out."

"Fine, you're right, fine. I'll start collecting boxes. I'll keep my ears peeled for anything about apartments opening up. And we'll do a girls' night. You want to go tonight?"

I should go because the thought of sitting here all night by myself is a little overwhelming, but I don't want to go out. I don't want to act like my life isn't falling apart, and I know my friends wouldn't expect me to, but I would feel like I should. "No, I think I'll stay in."

"Well, that's okay. The girls and I can come there. I'll bring pizza and ice cream... or do you feel more like having wine.... Ooh, or is it a tequila night?"

I take another sip of tea. "I'm sorry, Jilly. But tonight, I just want to be alone. I'm going to take a hot bath, maybe read a little bit and go to sleep. I'm giving myself tonight, and then tomorrow, I'll get back to it all."

"Are you sure, Nat? I hate to leave you..."

"I promise, I'm fine. I'll call you if I need anything. You know I will."

She sighs loudly into the phone. "Okay, I'll see you tomorrow in class, and if you're not there, I'm coming over."

I can't hold back my laugh. "I know you will. I love you, Jilly. Thanks for everything."

"Love you, Nat. I'll see you in the morning."

I hang up the phone and close the blind that leads to the backyard. I can't just sit here all day looking for a sight of my soon-to-be ex-husband.

I take my teacup to the kitchen and am washing it out when the doorbell rings. I freeze for just a second, trying to figure out who it could be. I know I'm being ridiculous. I set the cup down and make my way to the front door. Looking through the peephole, I see that it's Huddy, one of Beau's brothers.

I look in the mirror next to the door and instantly realize it's no use. My eyes are puffy, my hair standing up all over my head. There's no time to fix it. I pull open the door and force a smile to my face. "Hey, Huddy!"

He smiles broadly at me. "Natalie, hey there. How's it going?"

I lean against the half-opened door instead of opening it further. "It's good. I'm glad you're home, and I know Beau is too."

He looks at the door and then at me. "Is Beau here? When I heard he skipped out on work today, I thought I'd come by and see what he was up to."

I clench my hand on the door. Obviously, Beau hasn't told his brothers anything about us. "Well, he's here... but he's not here." I roll my eyes and suck in a breath, trying not to cry again. "He moved into the pool house."

"What? He moved into the pool house?"

I nod and suck in a deep breath. "Yeah, he's out at the pool house."

He's looking at me with curiosity, but I don't give him time to put voice to the question I know he wants to ask. I'm a fool, and the tears I've worked so hard to hold back start to flow. "I'm sorry," I tell him as I wipe at my cheeks. "Shoot, you don't need to see me fall apart. I'm fine. But yeah, if you want to go out back, I'm sure Beau would love to see you. I'll talk to you soon, Huddy. I'm glad you're home."

I close the door before I completely fall apart. It's only when I'm by myself again that I let myself give in to the tears. I told Jilly I was going to give myself tonight, and that's what I'm going to do. I'm going to cry until I can't cry anymore, and then tomorrow, I'm going to get my life together.

Chapter 5

Beau

There's a knock at the door, and for an instant, I wonder if it's Natalie. I close my laptop and take the three steps from the couch to open it.

When I swing open the door, I lean against it. I don't even try to hide my disappointment. "Oh, it's you."

Huddy is my older brother by two years, and he's spent the last twenty years in the military. He's only recently come home, and I'm glad to have him back even if I don't seem like it right now.

Huddy pushes past me through the door. "Yeah, it's me. What the fuck is going on, Beau?"

I don't act like I don't know what he's talking about because I'm sure he had to have seen Natalie to know I'm out here in my fuckin' pool house. I sit down on the couch and lean my arms onto my knees. "I'm getting a divorce. That's what is going on."

He nods and sits down across from me. Even though we've been apart for as long as we have, I know that look he's giving me. He's going to try and fix all this, and he doesn't understand that my marriage is not fixable. He claps his hands together. "Okay, so let's talk about it."

I blurt out a laugh. "Yeah, I'd rather not."

Huddy moves even further to the end of his seat. I'm almost afraid he's going to fall to the floor, he's so close to the edge. He clasps his hands together in front of him. "Well, fuck that, because we're talking about it. Are you okay?"

I give him a look like I can't believe he just asked me that. "Really? That's what you're asking me? My wife is divorcing me. How do you think I am?"

Huddy stands up and starts to pace back and forth in the small living area. "Okay, so look, I'm just wondering because I'm an outsider looking in, but I'm wondering if this isn't for the best."

I jump up from my seat. "This is for the best? Are you listening to yourself? This is my marriage you're talking about."

He crosses his arms over his chest. "I know that, but I also know that since I got back into town, you're not the same. I had to carry your drunk ass home the other night."

I nod my head because the truth is, I'm still feeling the effects from the other night. As the owner of a distillery, you would think I could handle my liquor a little better but obviously not. "Yeah, I knew then that something was up with Nat. She's been distancing herself for a while. I thought I could numb it all with some drinks, but you saw how that worked out."

"Okaaay, so hear me out. Natalie hasn't been to any of Ollie's soccer games. She doesn't come for family dinners, she doesn't want anything to do with your family. She—"

I cut him off. "She came to Granny's funeral... she insisted."

He walks over to the window and looks out at the pool. "What do you mean, she insisted?"

I open my mouth to answer and then close it quickly. How do I explain all this?

When I don't answer, he turns around. "Beau? What do you mean she insisted?"

I move into the kitchenette area and open the fridge. "Do you want a drink, Huddy? There's probably something in here. Maybe a water."

He comes to stand next to me. "Beau. Talk to me. What do you mean she insisted?"

I blow out a breath. I might as well come clean. I close the refrigerator door and stand up to my full height. "Natalie and I have been married for two years. In those two years, I've never invited her to a family function. Heck, I didn't even ask her to all the dinners or fundraisers we do with Blaze. I didn't invite her to Lucas and Issi's wedding, but she was friends with Issi and went on her own."

Huddy's eyes widen, and he jerks as if I've completely stumped him. "But why? Why have you not included her in anything? That doesn't even make sense, brother. You're a family guy. Heck, you love your family."

I nod and lean across the counter with my head in my hands. He's right. My family has always been important to me, and Nat's no different. But it's different with her. I made it different. "Huddy, look, I know what women are capable of. I know they leave. I wasn't going to have her become involved in my life and my family's life and then be devastated when it was time for her to go. I protected myself... and my family."

Huddy is staring at me with his mouth hanging open. "Are you serious right now? Just because our mother—"

I cut him off. "It's not just our mother. Yeah, she left us the day Lucas was born, but she's not the only one. Do you remember my fiancée I had my senior year of college? They all leave, Huddy. And yes, I wanted to marry Natalie. I love her. I wanted to keep her for however long she'd stay with me. But now she's leaving."

I say it so decisively as if I've already come to terms with it when in fact I feel like I'm drowning.

Huddy is shaking his head and holds his hand up. "Wait. Are you telling me that for the last two years, you have made sure not to include her in your family's life... in YOUR life? Is that what you're saying?"

"That's exactly right."

He starts to laugh. "And she put up with this for two years? Now what? She divorces you and gets half of everything you own?"

I feel as if I'm about to throw up. In a voice all void of emotion, I tell him the truth. "She doesn't want anything. The gym is already in her name. I had to force her to take her car. She doesn't want the house or any money. Hell, she was going to leave to go to a friend's house last night, but I made her stay in the house. She doesn't want anything from me."

Huddy stares at me in shock and then throws his hands up in the air. "You dumb son of a bitch. What the fuck were you thinking?" He stops and holds his hand up. "Wait. Forget it. Don't answer that because you obviously weren't thinking. Beau, answer me one thing."

I pinch my nose between my fingers and then rub my fingers over my eyes. "What is it, Huddy? What do you want to know?"

"Do. You. Love. Her?" He enunciates each word, and when I don't answer him, he asks again, "Do you love her? Answer me, Beau."

I choke on the answer, but I know I can't lie about it. "Yes. Okay, yes, I do love her."

He seems almost angry now. "And that's how you show her. You don't make her a part of the family? You make her an outsider like she's someone you're ashamed of or something. I can just imagine how she feels right now. She probably thinks none of us think she's good enough for you or some crazy shit like that. And now she wants a divorce. It's no damn surprise to me. How much do you think a woman can take?"

I shrug my shoulders as if I don't have a care in the world when in fact I haven't slept a wink all night and now I'm completely sick about all of it. "It doesn't matter, it's done."

"But it's not done, you fool. You can still make this right."

I'm shaking my head. "It's too late."

"Fuck, Beau. This is ridiculous. So you kept her at arm's length because you were scared to lose her, and now here we are. You're losing her. Does it hurt any less? Are you okay with watching her walk away?"

His words sink in, and it's like a weight on my chest. I can't breathe. I can't focus on anything. I close my eyes and see her big blue eyes looking back at me. I suck in a breath, but it doesn't help. "Fuuuuckkk!" I scream.

Huddy grabs me by the arms and shoves me against the counter. "Listen to me. Look at our father. If he had given up after Mom left, he never would have spent the last forty or so years with Charlotte. I've never seen Lucas as happy as he is now, and you know as well as I do, it's because of Issi. And fuck, look at Ford. His ex-wife completely fucked him and Ollie over. If someone should be scared of love, he should be, but look at him now. He and Ollie have Lilian. And me, I have Elle." He holds his hand up. "And yes, the thought of losing her absolutely guts me, but all I can do is work every day to make her happy so that she never even considers leaving me. I know as well as anyone that there's no guarantees, but living a life without Ellie is not an option."

"Fuck, I know Huddy. I know."

He comes to stand next to me. "You have to do something."

I nod my head. "But what? I fucked up for two years. She wants out. How do I even come back from this?"

He claps me on the back. "I'll tell you what you do. You man the fuck up, brother. You need to make a plan and then do whatever you have to do, but you don't let her leave."

Just a flare of hope starts to ignite inside me, and I know he's right. All I've thought about all night is that I can't picture my life without her in it. I fucked up, and I can't imagine her forgiving me, but I'm going to do everything I can to make her change her mind.

Chapter 6

Natalie

Can we have dinner tonight? I would like to talk.

That's the text I got from Beau this morning. It took me an hour to respond but mostly because I had to convince myself that I could handle it. Last night, I did exactly what I told Jilly I would do. I cried, took a bath, and lay in bed trying to figure out my next step. This morning, I went and taught class and then had lunch with Jilly and the girls where we talked about everything except my impending divorce. Of course, Jilly knows, but I haven't told the others yet. Now I'm sitting here, waiting on Beau to show up.

It's still early, and he's not supposed to be here for another half hour, and if history is any indication, he'll probably be late, but here I sit, ready and anxiously waiting.

I jump out of my chair when there's a knock on the door twenty minutes before he's supposed to be here. I open the door to my husband and try to hide my surprise. Instead of the suit and tie, he's in his jeans. His normally clean-shaven face is covered in scruff, and the reserved look that is a constant on his face seems more relaxed. "Hey." I point at the door. "Did you just knock on the door? At your own house?"

He looks almost sheepish. "Yeah, I wasn't sure and didn't want to upset you."

I nod. Maybe he's right. We should have some boundaries, and I guess it's only right that until this is officially over, we have some rules set in place. I open the door farther. "Right. Can I help you with anything? I could have just cooked."

He walks in the house, his eyes traveling up and down my body before he bites his lip and grimaces. "Nope, I got it. I didn't want you to have to cook."

I follow behind him. "Right. I know you never really cared for my cooking—"

He cuts me off and stops so suddenly, I run into his back. With my hands on the back of his arms, I push away from him. He turns and stares down at me. "I love your cooking. I just always felt bad that you worked all day and then had to come home to cook, that's all."

I cross my arms over my chest. "You hired someone to come and cook because..."

I let my voice trail off, and he takes a step toward me. "Because I knew I couldn't cook, and I didn't think you cared one way or another. I thought..." He stops and sighs, shaking his head. "I thought I was doing something good for you."

I reach for one of the bags in his hand, trying not to touch him as I do so, but inevitably, my hand touches his. I bite onto my lip and move past him into the dining room. I set down the bag, and we both work on taking things out. I lift the familiar container and open it. "Really? Is it that kind of talk? You thought you needed to bring my favorite?"

He huffs out a breath. "There's a lot we need to talk about, Nat. And I brought your favorite because I wanted to see you smile."

And just like that, a smile forms on my lips. "There, I'm smiling. But how can I not, when I'm holding a piece of Red's cinnamon Apple Blaze cake?"

He opens another Styrofoam container and holds it up. "Well, don't miss your favorite comfort meal. Meat loaf, macaroni and cheese, and green beans."

I stare between the container and him in surprise. "It is my favorite." I grab the plate from him and go and sit down in my seat. Instead of the seat he usually sits in at the far end of the table, he sits down in the seat next to me and opens his container.

I stand up. "I'll grab plates."

He puts his hand on mine to keep me where I'm at. "No, we can eat on these. It's fine."

I try not to let him see my surprise as I set back down. I take a bite of the food and moan. At lunch today, I barely ate, and for the first time since yesterday, I'm really hungry.

We eat in silence for a few minutes, and the calm feeling I usually feel when we're together is gone. I pat my stomach. "I'll have to fit in an extra workout this week because I plan on eating that whole piece of cake."

He looks at my body and smiles. "You're perfect, Nat, just the way you are."

I try not to let the compliment go to my head because the fact remains we're getting a divorce.

I eat a few more bites and then push my plate away. Suddenly, my hunger is gone. "So you said you wanted to talk tonight."

He nods as he pushes his plate away too. "Yeah, I was hoping we could talk about what you said last night."

I sigh. "About the divorce."

He openly cringes and nods his head. "Yeah. I don't want to get a divorce."

For just a second, I feel hopeful, and then when I realize that nothing has changed in the last twenty-four hours, I know that I need to go through with it. "It's too late, Beau. I think we said everything we needed to say last night. I want a divorce."

He opens the container that holds his cake and takes a bite of it. He looks as if he doesn't have a care in the world as he savors the bite he just took. It's only when he shakes his head and opens his eyes that I can see the hard look on his face letting me know my words have any effect on him. "But that's just it, Nat. I don't want a divorce. I don't want to let you go."

I cross my legs under the table and lean back in my seat with my arms crossed over my chest. "Well, it seems we want two different things, Beau."

He licks the icing off his fork, and I can't take my eyes off his tongue. That's something I'm definitely going to miss.

He sets the fork down and narrows his eyes at me. "Last night, I asked you if there was someone else."

I open my mouth, and he holds his hand up. "You hesitated. Whether you realize it or not, you hesitated. Is. There. Someone. Else?"

I uncross my arms on my chest and settle them on the table in front of me as I lean forward. "Beau, I've never cheated on you."

His forehead creases. "But? I hear a but in there."

I shake my head. "I haven't cheated on you, and I wouldn't. The reason I hesitated is because there is a man—"

He cuts me off. "Who is it?"

I shrug. "It doesn't matter. He knows I'm married, and he knows I'm not interested, but I'm not going to lie to you. It feels good that he finds me attractive and he flirts with me."

His jaw hardens. "He flirts with you?"

I throw my hands up in the air. "It doesn't matter. He's just some guy at the gym. He has nothing to do with us or my decision to end our marriage. You asked why I hesitated, and it's because even though I've never done anything nor would I, I do feel guilty that another man makes me feel attractive. That's it."

"I think you're attractive. I think you're the most beautiful woman I've ever seen."

I should keep my mouth closed. There's no reason to argue about this, but I can't stop myself. "Really? Is that why you only touch me when we're in our bedroom? Is that why you never want to be seen with me? Hell, Beau, some people don't even know I'm your wife. Whiskey Run is small, and everyone knows everyone, but there are people that have no idea that you have a wife... that I'm your wife."

He's shaking his head, obviously not listening to a word I say. "We're not getting a divorce, Nat."

I give him a half-hearted shrug. "Well, then I don't know where we go from here because we obviously disagree on things."

He gets out of his seat and paces back and forth behind me. I sit quietly as he seems to get lost in thought. The piece of cake I was looking forward to sits uneaten.

I lean my head on the back of the chair and close my eyes, and even now, I wonder if I'm making the right decision. I love Beau, but I can't continue like this. I already feel like I've lost who I am. It's time I put myself first.

I lift my head when he sits back down and scoots his chair closer to me. "Can we talk about this?"

I try to stay strong and avoid eye contact. "Sure, we can talk about it, but I don't think it's going to change anything."

He reaches across the table and grabs my hand. I watch as he laces our fingers together. With his other hand, he rubs his thumb across my knuckles. "Will you do me a favor?"

I should say no. I know that I should, but just as I open my mouth to say it, I mutter, "What kind of favor?"

"I want you to do something for me."

He grips my hand tighter, and I force the words out. "What do you want?"

"Give me a month...."

His voice trails off, and when he doesn't continue, I ask him, "Give you a month for what?"

"I'm taking a month off work. I had a meeting with my brothers today. Huddy and Elle are going to take over the CFO duties for me."

Speechless, my mouth falls open, and he laughs. "I know, I never take any time off, and it sounds crazy to think I'm taking a month off, but I am."

I look at our joined hands. "And what are you going to do this month? What do you want from me?"

"I want you to go to Ollie's soccer games with me. Maybe he can spend the night here with us one night. I want you to come to our family dinners. I have a fundraiser coming up, and I'd like you to go with me. Lucas and Issi's baby is due this month, and

I want you to be there with me when he or she is born. Ford and Lilian are getting married. I'm sure Huddy and Elle will be next. I want you to go with me."

"Beau, that's not all happening in a month."

His posture is rigid, and his forearms are flexed. "Maybe not, but whatever does happen in the month, I want you to be there with me. I realized that I've messed up, and I want to make it right."

If he had asked me this last week, I would have given him a resounding yes. It wasn't until after we married that I realized he planned to keep our lives separate. Originally, he just never asked me, and when I confronted him about it, he would apologize, but he still didn't ask me the next time or the time after that. I never understood it just like I never understood how he could be so cold about things like that, but then other ways he would be caring and loving. I think about his request. In the past, I would have given anything to be a part of his family, but what's the point now? "I don't think that's a good idea, Beau. I'm sorry... but I can't."

He turns my chair toward him, grips my thighs, and pulls me toward him. His legs are wide, fitting mine between his. His knees lock against my sides, and his hands go to my arms. "Look at me."

I don't listen to him. I keep my head lowered, not wanting to look in his face because I know I'm weak when it comes to him. "Natalie, I want you to look at me."

I lift my head and jut my chin at him. "What? I'm looking at you. Now what?"

He smiles at me. "I know I'm asking for a lot."

I nod. "Yes, you are. For the last two years, you've treated me like your little secret instead of your wife, so excuse me if I'm not jumping at whatever game this is you're playing."

He releases his hold on my arms and instead wraps his hands around my thighs. "I'm not playing any games."

"Right."

His jaw tightens, and he grinds his teeth together. I can see the wheels turning as he looks at me. Finally, he breaks the silence. "I understand you don't trust me, and if you can't give me a month, just give me a chance. We can take it day by day."

I'm leaning as far back in my chair as I can, but it's not enough. I'm not going to make good decisions with him this close to me. He's a temptation that I can't refuse. I stare at his lips, and it's like a movie plays in my head of all the times he's satisfied me with them. "Day by day. If I do that, will you let me up?"

He rears back in surprise and releases me instantly. I jump up out of my seat and walk around to put the table between us. "I'll give you that. Day by day, but that's all I can promise. No sex either."

He nods and runs his hand through his hair. "Okay. I won't have sex with you unless you ask me to. And we take this day by day." He doesn't seem completely happy with the agreed terms, but at least he's willing. "I'll see you in the morning, wife."

With a shaky hand, I grab the back of the chair. "I teach in the morning."

He cleans up the table, and when he's done, he points at the untouched piece of cake. "Eat your cake. Sleep well, wife."

I stare at him the whole way as he walks through the house and out the back door. I'm not sure what to make of any of this, but I let myself eat the piece of cake and replay the night's events in my head. I'm not sure, but I'm thinking my husband has a plan to date me.

Chapter 7

Beau

I *will not kill the guy. I will not kill the guy.*

That's what I'm telling myself as I walk into Work It Out, Nat's gym. I made a point to show up right after her class was over. As the people are coming out of the cycling room, the women all are looking at me as they walk by, but I keep my eye on the door.

Nat is the last one out of the room, and I walk up to her. She is wiping her face with a towel, and when she finally spots me, she stops mid stride, and her mouth falls open. She has on some kind of tight black leggings and a small tank top that does nothing to hide her body. She's beautiful. I know it, and I'm sure every man in the gym knows it too. I want to look at each of them and dare them to look at her, but I don't. I keep my eyes glued on Nat. "Morning," I say gruffly.

If anything, her eyes get even bigger. "Morning."

Normally, that would be it. I'm not a man that shows affection, but I'm determined to give this all I've got. Last night, I thought about what she said, and it blows my mind that she thought I could be embarrassed by her. I lean over until our faces are inches apart. "You look good, wife." I planned to leave it at that, but her full lips are beckoning me. I kiss her lightly and force myself to pull back even though every cell in my body wants to find a private room to take her to.

She reaches up and presses her fingertips to her lips. "What are you doing here?"

I shrug. "Well, I need to find something to occupy my time, and I'm getting a little flabby sitting at my desk all the time. I thought I'd come and work out."

She looks at me, her eyes moving slowly down my body and then back up again. "You're getting flabby? You don't have an ounce of fat on your body, Beau."

I shrug and try not to let the way she's staring at me affect me. All I need is to have a raging hard-on right in the middle of her gym. Almost sheepishly, I tell her, "I don't know. I thought it would be fun if we could work out together..."

She points between the two of us. "You want us to work out... together?"

I nod. "Yes, I do. But if you'd rather not—"

I stop when her smile absolutely lights up her whole face, telling me that I made the right decision in coming here today. She does some kind of little jump up and down, and I'm an ass because I instantly stare at her breasts. She puts her hand on my arm. "Okay, you get started. I'm going to go get cleaned up a little, and I'll be back."

She walks away just a few steps and turns around. "I'll be right back."

I laugh. "I'm not going anywhere."

I watch her walk away, and it's not until she's through the door that leads to the back that I look around the gym. There are a few women working out and a few men over at the free weights area. I walk over to the opposite end of the room and find an empty cable machine. I normally work out with my brothers at a gym with no frills. I'm surprised at how nice this one is. I want to kick myself that I haven't been in here since right after she opened.

I'm pulling at a weight when she comes back into the gym. She's changed into blue leggings and a matching top. Her eyes seem to sparkle when she finds me, and she comes to stand next to me. "Looking good, Mr. Blaze."

I grunt as I pull another rep. I put on more weight than I should have, but with her looking at me the way she does, I seem to have renewed strength. I count out another rep of ten and let the weight go. "This place is nice, Nat. Really nice. I'm impressed."

She preens under my praise, and her blush has her turning away. She goes to a machine next to me and starts a rep of arm curls.

It's when I'm watching her that I see a man in the mirror looking our way. He's a big guy, heck, bigger than Huddy, but the way he's looking at my wife gives me no doubt I could take him if I need to.

I try to ignore him, but there's no mistaking the way he keeps looking at Nat.

She doesn't seem to notice. Her attention is on me, even giving me shit on my form as I do reps on my tricep press-downs.

I will not kill him. I will not kill him. I go back to my silent mantra that I had when I walked in here, but it's not doing anything to help calm me. I try to concentrate on Nat and her working out beside me but keep one eye on the man in the mirror. It's him. I don't need Nat to tell me because I know. He's the one that has been flirting with my wife.

A rage like I've never felt fills me. I try to keep my cool and focus on my beautiful wife. But knowing there's a man that wants what is mine is my undoing.

I walk over to the machine that Nat is working on. I trail my hand across her shoulder. She gives me a strange look, and I know I shouldn't, but there's no stopping me now. "Is that him?" I gesture to the man in the mirror who is looking this way.

Instead of answering me, Nat shakes her head. "Really? Is that what this is about, Beau? You couldn't stand that some man is flirting with me, so you show up here to check it out? What are you going to do, piss on me and mark your territory?"

She's hissing at me, and even though she started off quietly, the more she says, the louder she gets. I shake my head. "It's not like that. I'm here—"

She cuts me off before I can finish. "And now you're leaving."

She walks off, and I watch her go. Everything inside me wants to grab her and take her right here where I stand, but I know that's not the answer. That's not even what this is about. I'm here to win her back, and already I've fucked it up.

She closes the door as she walks into the office. There's a window, but it's only one way. She can see out, but people can't see in. Before I can even come up with a plan, I'm on the move. I walk into her office, and she's sitting behind her desk. She looks exhausted as she looks up at me. "Beau, please, I've had enough."

I shut the door behind me, hold my hands up, and try to calm my breathing. "I know what it looks like, me showing up here when I've never come before. I'm a dumbass, Nat. That's the truth."

She crosses her arms over her chest. "Yes, you are."

I smile and hold my hand out to her. "Come here."

She shakes her head side to side. "No, I'm good over here."

"I didn't come here because of him." I point out the window, and sure enough, the man keeps glancing this way. "I came here because of you. We're going to do this, Nat. Day by day."

She fidgets with the pencil in her hands before tapping it on the desk. "I know, I agreed to day by day, but I didn't agree to this, and you coming here because you're jealous is just ridiculous."

"This isn't because I'm jealous."

She blurts out a laugh. "Yeah, right."

I hold my hand out again. "Do you trust me, Nat?"

She makes a big deal of rolling her eyes at me. "You know I do."

I keep my feet planted where I'm at but stick my hand out even farther. It's important that she comes to me. "Come here."

She blows out a breath and comes toward me. She reaches for my hand, and I hold it as I pull her closer.

I put her in front of me and point out the window. "Look."

She doesn't look out the window, though; she looks at me. "Beau, it's not—"

I put my finger on her chin and turn it so she's looking out the window. "Look."

She looks out the window, and I know she sees the man looking this way. "I see the way he looks at you."

She tries to pull from my arms, but I hold her tighter, not letting her go. "No, stay, hear me out." In a rush, I continue, "I see the way he looks at you. He knows you're beautiful, and he probably dreams of having you. What man wouldn't?"

Her breathing picks up, and I put one hand at her waist, drawing her back against my body. My cock is hard, and there's no doubt she feels it against her backside. "Me coming here today is not to stake my claim. I know you wouldn't cheat on me. Me coming here is to show you that I'm no longer taking you for granted. I think you're beautiful, but I didn't say it enough... I didn't show you enough. All that's going to change now."

I lean down and brush my lips along her cheek. "That guy—fuck, every guy is going to look at you and wish you were his. But what I want is that when they look at you, I want you to think of me."

I let my hand trail down her stomach beneath the waistband of her leggings. She grabs onto it and holds it in place. Her body tremors with every breath she takes. "We agreed. No sex."

I bury my nose into her shoulder and take a shuddering breath. "I'm not asking you for sex, Nat. I'm asking if I can make you come."

Her chest expands as she takes a deep breath and lets it out slowly. I could move my hand between her thighs and convince her that this is what she wants, but I need her to want it. Her hips lift in the slightest way, and I smile. "You want this, don't you?"

She nods her head, and where her hand is still holding mine, she moves it farther down until I'm palming her mound. I stroke a finger through her wet slit, and she leans her head back, resting it on my shoulder. I circle my finger around her clit, and when she moans, I apply more pressure. With one hand between her thighs, I pull her sports bra up to let her breasts free. I take turns kneading each one, and she's so close. Her pussy is hot and wet, and I don't want it to be over yet.

I turn my head and kiss her neck, her cheek, and then her lips. I pull away, and she leans up, not wanting me to let go. "Lift your head up, baby. Look."

She lifts her head up and looks at me, and I gesture to the window. The man is still looking this way, and Nat tenses in my arms. "No, no, don't tense up on me. I'm not punishing you. I'm going to make you come, baby. But from now on, when he flirts with you and tries to get to know you, I want you to think about this right here. I want you to think about how much I want you. How I'm hard any time I think about you." I nudge my hips against her, pressing my hard cock against her ass. "I want you to know that no matter what, I'm the one that wants to make your dreams come true. I'm the one that wants to pleasure you and make you come."

She loops her arm up around my neck, and I feel her nails dig into my skin. All it does is push me further. "He can look all he wants to, Nat. I can't blame him for it. But he better never touch you because you're mine. I won't let you go, and if I have to come here every day to prove to you I have everything you'll ever need, that's what I'll do. You're mine."

Her body starts to jerk, but I don't stop. Her pussy clamps around my hand, but I don't stop rubbing her until she's writhing in my arms, grunting my name over and over. The orgasm takes over her body, but I don't stop until she goes limp in my arms. I move us over to a chair and sit down with her pulled into my lap. She rests her head against my chest, and I try to control my breathing. I'm so fucking hard, and my cock is leaking in my shorts, but none of that matters right now.

I lift the hand that was between her legs and bring it to my mouth. I suck my fingers, moaning around the flavor that hits my tongue. She tastes good, and it only excites me further. I want nothing more than to bend her over her desk and take her now, but I know I can't. I haven't earned that right yet, but I plan to.

When her breaths even out, I kiss her forehead. "Have dinner with me tonight."

I wait for her to argue with me or list all the reasons why it's a bad idea, but she just shrugs her shoulders. "Tonight is book club."

I nod, trying not to show my disappointment. Today is only day one of trying to win my wife back, and I'm making some headway. I'm willing to be patient. I help her out of my lap as I try to put her clothes back where they belong. "I'm going to get out of here. I know you need to work."

She gestures to the bulge between my legs, and I grab her hand before she touches me. The truth is, I'm barely hanging on, and I don't want to come in my shorts. "I'm fine... or I will be fine."

She nods, looking out the window and then back at me. "I'm sorry about... him. I don't want him... I never did."

I nod and try to keep my cool about it all. "I know that, Nat." I brush a piece of her blond hair off her face. "And I'm going to make sure I keep it that way. You need anything, no matter what it is, you come to me."

She nods slowly, and I kiss her lightly on the lips. "I'll see you later."

She opens her mouth and closes it again as she nods her head.

I force myself to walk away. I pull her office door closed behind me, and the sound has the man looking at me. I pause to give him a look that tells him I know what he's up to. It's crude, but I give him a satisfied smile and adjust my cock in my shorts. He looks away, and my smile gets even bigger as I walk past him toward the door. Nat is mine, and I'm going to do whatever I have to do to keep her.

Chapter 8

Natalie

I'm holding my sides, rocking back and forth. My cheeks are hurting from laughing so hard, but it's like this any time I get together with my book club. You would think we'd learn our lesson and have our meetings in a private location because we always end up drawing the attention of everyone in the bar or restaurant. Jilly, Abby, Olivia, Chloe, who couldn't make it tonight, and I get together to talk about the book we're currently reading, and usually it turns into a discussion about our lives, loves, and orgasms.

Yeah, right now, Olivia is excited about her new idea. She wants us to do a book club field trip and go to a sex club to see what they're all about. Just imagining it has us all rolling in laughter.

I'm shaking my head as I look around the Whistler. For a weekday night, it's pretty busy. It's the only bar in town—well, there are two if you count the biker bar at the edge of town. I lean over and whisper loudly to Olivia, "We're not going to a sex club. No way."

She rolls her eyes. "Whatever, you're getting dick on the regular. Speak for yourself. The rest of us have to work a little harder for it."

Jilly's mouth is open, and I know she's planning to defend me or maybe even tell them about my impending divorce. Normally, I tell these women everything that's happening in my life, but right now, I don't want to talk about it. I grab a French fry out of the basket and shove it in Jilly's open mouth to keep her quiet. With a stern look and a shake of my head, she gets the picture.

I know she won't sell me out, but she does make a big dramatic roll of her eyes about the fry I stuffed in her mouth. She pulls it out with a choke. "Really, Nat? You know I'm trying to cut back on carbs, and what do you do? Force feed me. I mean, come on."

She takes a big bite of the French fry, and Olivia jumps in. "Right, if you're going to stuff your mouth, you should stuff it with c-o-c-k."

She spells it out, but she does it loudly, and the people at the tables around are looking our way. I can feel my face heat, and I shush my friends. "Guys, seriously, can we please have a meeting that is not going to be the talk of the town by morning? From now on, we have to meet somewhere private."

Abby laughs too and looks around the table. "Okay, okay, let's talk about the book. What did you guys think?"

Jilly scrunches her nose up. "Too much sex."

Olivia looks offended and sputters, "Not enough sex."

Abby shrugs her shoulders. "I don't know. I thought that part of it was fine, but I just don't think there was any connection at all. I mean, I have trouble believing they're in love. I just wasn't buying it."

Olivia and Jilly nod their heads in agreement, and before I know it, I have three pairs of eyes on me. Olivia is the first to ask me, "What about you, Nat? What'd you think?"

Abby is next, and she narrows her eyes at me. "You didn't read it, did you?"

I suck in a breath and nod my head. "I read it."

Jilly is looking at me with pity, and she opens her mouth. I know she's about to save me. She'll do something to take the attention off me because that's the kind of friend she is, but before she gets the words out, I say it. I say what I've been thinking since I first sat down. Hell, what I've been thinking about nonstop. "I asked Beau for a divorce."

Jilly reaches for me, covering my hand with hers, and both Olivia and Abby gasp. They knew that my marriage wasn't the best, but I'm not sure they knew it was this bad.

And just like that, all talk of the book is over. Abby leans in. "What happened, Nat? I don't understand."

I roll my eyes. "Come on, you guys noticed. You had to. I mean, have you ever seen us at a fundraiser, dinner, heck at a store together? You never saw him at my gym... We have completely separate lives, and I guess I'm over it."

Abby slams her hand on the table. Of all of us, Abby is the quiet one, and she always remains calm, so when she makes a loud noise, we all take notice. "It's his loss, Nat. You're amazing, and if he doesn't see that, then it's his problem."

Olivia is nodding her head and joins in. "Yes, exactly. You deserve to be happy, and I'll be honest, Nat, you don't seem happy and haven't for some time."

I'm nodding along because what she's saying is the truth. I haven't been happy for a while. Not really.

I look at Jilly. Of all my friends, she's heard it all, and she knows all my insecurities. I smile nervously at her. "What about you? You got anything to say?"

A cheer breaks out across the bar followed by a round of laughter, but my three friends keep their eyes glued on me. I grip my hands together, waiting for Jilly to respond.

She's hesitant. "You know that no matter what I'm on your side, Natalie. There's no doubt about that."

She stops speaking, but it's obvious she has something else she wants to say.

"But..." I prompt.

She shakes her head. "No, there are no buts. I stand behind you on whatever you want to do."

I lean over the table. "But you think I'm doing the wrong thing?"

She scrunches her nose up and shakes her head. "I didn't say that."

The silence between us is palpable as we stare at each other. Olivia and Abby are turning their heads, looking between the two of us, but they both remain silent. I lean toward her. "You're not saying a lot."

She blows out a breath and tilts her head to the side. "Do you love him?"

"Jilly, what kind of question—"

She interrupts me by holding her hand up in front of my face. "Stop. Answer me, do you love him?"

I glare at her. "You know I do."

She nods, uncrosses her legs, and scoots to the end of her stool. "Okay, so you love him. Why do you want a divorce?"

I huff out a breath. She knows the answer to this, but I repeat my reasoning to her. "You know why. We have separate lives, and he likes it that way. He's emotionally cut off, the only time he touches me—

hell, acts as if we're even married—is when we're home behind closed doors."

She nods because she's heard this all before. "Right, and why does he do that? Why is he like that?"

I practically rip the napkin in my hand apart. "Because he's embarrassed by me."

She juts her chin at me. "Bullshit."

I throw my hands in the air. "Bullshit? Really? What else could it be? He doesn't act as if we're married in front of anyone. No secret touches, no holding hands, nothing. What other reason could there be?"

She leans forward and covers my hand with hers. "I understand how frustrating that is, Nat. Especially since you're such a touchy-feely person, but have you ever thought that you should ask him?"

My hand fists under hers. This whole thing is embarrassing really. There's nothing like admitting to your best friends that your husband is embarrassed to be seen with you. "Why would I ask him? It's obvious that he doesn't want to be seen with me."

Her hand tightens on mine. "I think you're letting your feelings cloud the facts. He loves you, Nat. It's obvious to anyone that's been around you that he cares for you. And yeah, maybe he doesn't show you affection in front of others, but maybe that's just who he is. There are a lot of people that don't like public displays of affection."

I shake my head. "It's not just the fact he won't hold my hand, Jilly. He doesn't want me involved with his family. All the get-togethers, dinners, Ollie's soccer games, all of it. He doesn't invite me. Heck, he wasn't going to invite me to Issi and Lucas' wedding, but Issi did."

"Why?"

I pull my hand out from under hers. I'm over this conversation. I expected my friends to be on my side, but Jilly doesn't seem to see things my way. "Just forget it. Let's get back to the book."

She shakes her head. "No, answer me. We've talked about this for months, Natalie, and my question is the same. Why? Why would a man that obviously loves you—he would literally give you the world— why would he act like this?"

I suck in a breath and at the same time, try to hold back a sob. "I don't know. Hell, I feel like I don't know anything anymore."

She wraps her hand around my wrist and holds on to me. I lift my eyes from the table in front of me and look at my best friend. I've never doubted our friendship. I know she is a good friend, and I know she means well. Just like I know she expects me to answer. "I don't know."

She nods her head, and her hand tightens on me. "I know you don't, honey. You need to talk to him. You need to communicate. And yes, I know you're not happy, but are you ready to give him up forever without knowing all the facts? Talk to him, tell him how you feel, and see what he has to say."

I search her eyes. She makes it sound so easy, but can it really be that simple?

But Jilly is not done. "All I'm saying is that he holds the answers, Nat. You need to ask him, and then when you know all the facts, then you make your decisions for the future."

Jilly gives me hope when for the last few months, I've had none. All this time, I thought he wanted to keep our marriage hidden, but maybe there could be another reason. He told me last night that he wasn't embarrassed by me, but what else could he say? Could it be that simple that I just need to ask him and he could maybe clear it all up with one answer? I'm so lost in thought, I barely hear Jilly until she waves her hand in front of my face. "Yeah?" I murmur.

She gives me a soft smile. "All I'm saying is that before you make a big decision like this, you want to be absolutely sure. Just talk to him. See what he says."

I nod. "You're right. Fuck, you're right, Jilly. I'll talk to him." I make the promise to her, but at the same time I'm wondering if I'll get the chance. I literally told him I wanted a divorce. If he wanted to, he could walk away now without looking back.

I suck in a breath and let it out slowly. "Okay, so this calls for more than a Coke. I'm going to get a shot of tequila. Anyone want one?"

I'm up out of my seat and standing on shaky legs as I look at each one of them. I'm forcing a smile to my face, hoping to hide the pain, and they each nod their head. Jilly pats me on the back. "Go ahead. Catch a breath, go to the bathroom. I'll grab the drinks."

I nod a thank you to her and take off. Of course, Jilly knew I needed a little space and time to get myself together. As I walk into the bathroom, I go straight to the mirror and stare at my reflection. Before I can second-guess myself, I open my phone and send a text to Beau. *I'm in. Thirty days.*

I don't have to wait long for him to respond. *Thank you, Nat. You won't regret it. I love you, honey. Be safe tonight and let me know if you need a ride home.*

I type out a text but stop before I send it. *Do you really love me?*

I read the line three times before I start hitting the button to delete it. It doesn't have to be worked out all in one night. I've given us thirty days, and hopefully in that time, I can figure out what my next step needs to be. And even now, after everything, I can't picture my future without Beau in it.

Chapter 9

Beau

Go to lunch with me.

I send the text to Natalie as I sit outside her gym.

I stayed up until she got home last night. I was alerted by the cameras when she pulled into the driveway. I watched as the garage door came up and she pulled her car in and the door closed. It was only once I knew she was home, safe and sound, that I was able to turn the lights out and lie down in the bed.

I tossed and turned most of the night. I wanted to be lying next to Nat, where I belong. I've been so stupid. I've wasted so much time keeping her at a distance and thinking I'd be okay if she left me. I should have realized when I married her that the idea I could guard my heart was useless. I'm completely in love with her, and the thought of a future without her has made me physically sick.

I stare at my phone, waiting for the bubbles to pop up that she's texting me back.

I timed my text to send when I knew her class was over.

I let out a breath when the bubbles appear and then shortly after, a text.

It's ten in the morning.

I laugh and type out a response. *Fine, breakfast, brunch... whatever.*

I look through the window of the gym, hoping for just a glimpse of her, but when I don't see her, I stare down at my phone.

Give me a few minutes to get cleaned up. Meet me at Sugar Glaze Bakery?

YES.

I then take the next three minutes, watching the clock on the dashboard of my car. When it gets to two minutes remaining, I'm out of my SUV, pacing out front of Work It Out. I had intentions to play it cool and just meet her at the bakery, but I want more time with her. Hell, I want all the time with her, so I wait for her to come out so we can walk to the bakery together.

She comes out of her gym, wide-eyed. "Hey, I thought we were meeting at the bakery."

I shrug, reaching for her hand. She tenses, but she doesn't pull away. "I thought we could walk together. If you have time, there's a book fair in the square. We could go there after."

She stops and looks up at me. "You want to go to a book fair?"

Offended, I lift my shoulders. "I read."

She laughs and starts walking again. "Oh, I know you read. You're probably the smartest person I know. But this is a used book fair, and it's known for having romance books, children's books, and things like that. They don't usually have textbooks or hardly any nonfiction books."

I pull her closer to my side. "That's fine. You like to read romance."

She seems surprised. "Yeah, I do."

I nod my head at a person passing by and nudge Nat with my shoulder. "What? You don't think I know what you read?"

She avoids my gaze and is looking at the pavement in front of us. "I mean, I thought you might, but we never talked about it. You never asked me about it or anything."

I stop walking, and since we're holding hands, I pull her to stop next to me. I release my hold on her, but just for an instant. I palm her shoulders and take a step toward her until I can feel her pressed against the front of me. Already, my manhood is stirring, but I don't dare let go. "I know I've screwed up, Nat. Fuck, I almost lost you because of how I've behaved. I'm a fool, but I promise you I'm going to do better."

She finally lifts her eyes to mine, and she's looking at me skeptically. I've never lied to her, but I don't blame her for looking at me the way she is. Already in the span of just a few minutes, I've been more attentive and affectionate to her than I have in our whole marriage. Why should she believe me? I lean down until our lips are mere inches apart. "Trust me, Nat. Give me another chance."

She takes a step back, and I drop my hands from her shoulders. My heart nearly plummets to my stomach, and I'm about to reach for her when she grabs my hand. "Thirty days, Beau. We're going to try this for thirty days, and if it doesn't work, then we walk away."

She starts to turn, but I stop her. "Could you just walk away, Nat? Would it be that easy?"

She shakes her head and drags in a breath. Her chin quivers, but she seems to pull herself together. "No, it wouldn't be easy. It would be the hardest thing I've ever had to do."

Satisfied, I lean down and kiss her lightly on the lips before doing the same to her forehead. I wrap an arm around her and pull her tight against my body. "That's good, Nat. Because letting you go would be the hardest thing I've ever had to do."

We walk the rest of the way to the bakery in silence. As soon as we're inside, I point to a corner booth. "Have a seat. I'll get us some food."

Her eyes widen, but she nods her head and goes to sit down. I'm third in line, and when I get to the front, I order, pay, and watch as the woman behind the counter places my items on plates. She has to go back to the back to get a fresh batch of apple fritters, and I turn to look at Nat, hoping to catch her eye.

My hands fist at my sides, and the smile on my face drops when I see the man at the next table talking to Nat.

She's smiling and nodding her head, and I keep my eyes glued on her until the woman places the fritter on the tray and says, "That's everything, sir. You need anything else?"

I grumble, "Thank you," and her eyes widen at the tone of my voice. I smile, hoping to soften my tone and then stalk over to the table. I set the tray down, and before taking a seat, I lean over, pulling Nat's head back to kiss her thoroughly. Her moan of satisfaction has me pulling away. My cock is hard, but I force myself to sit across from her and then glare at the man at the next table. He gets the picture fast, smirks at me, and then loads his tray up with his trash. "It was nice talking to you, Natalie. I may see you at the gym soon."

She nods and smiles at him before turning to me. With her hands on the table, she leans forward and whispers loudly, "What was that all about?"

Her lips are swollen from our kiss, and all it does is make me want to kiss her again, but by the death glare she's giving me, I know she'd be resistant. "Has it always been like this?"

She leans in closer, still whispering, "Has what always been like this?"

I reach for her hand and lace our fingers together. "Everywhere you go, men hit on you..."

She pulls her hand from mine. "Is that what this is, Beau? You don't want me until you find out someone else does? If that's the case..."

I cross my arms on the table to stop myself from reaching for her. "That's not the case. I've always wanted you. I should have known, though, that men were into you like this. I should have paid better attention."

She shrugs and leans back in her seat. "What does it matter? Just because men flirt with me doesn't mean that I'm into it. I would never—"

I cut her off before she finishes. "I know you wouldn't, but that's not the point. All this time, and I've had no idea. I haven't treated you right, Nat."

She takes a deep breath. I know she wants to say something, but she's holding back. "So are we going to eat? I'm starving."

I want to ask her what she's thinking. It's obvious her thoughts are weighing heavily on her shoulders, but since she changed the subject, I don't want to push. Not yet. "Well, dig in. I got you the quiche Florentine and of course, your favorite, the apple fritter."

She looks at everything on the tray and smiles. "I can't eat all this. I'd have to work out for five hours to burn all those calories."

She picks up her fork and takes a small bite of the quiche. She's eyeing the fritter as she chews the egg and cheese. It's obvious by the look on her face what she'd rather be eating.

I pick up one of the two fritters, and her eyes follow as I take a big bite, chew, and swallow. "You know that I love your body."

She starts to choke but recovers quickly, putting a hand to her chest. "Excuse me?"

I shrug. "I know you enjoy eating healthy and working out, but I thought I should tell you. It seems that there are a lot of things I haven't told you, and I need to fix that. I. Love. Your. Body. I love everything about it. I love the curves of your hips, the softness of your belly, I love the way you fit in my arms as if you were made just for me. I love everything about you, Nat."

She drops her fork to the plate and looks at me with a tear in her eye. "You love me?"

My mouth falls open. What the fuck? Surely, I've told her I love her. I know I have. I think back to the last time I said it, and I can't remember. I can't fucking remember. Oh my God. "Nat, honey, of course I love you. I obviously haven't said it enough, but I'm going to fix that now." I get up and move around the table and get on one knee in front of her. I cup her face in my hands. "Honey, I love you more than anything. I'm sorry that I haven't said it, and I'm sorry that you obviously have doubted my love for you, but I do. I'm going to say it... fuck, I'm going to show you. You'll never doubt me again."

Her arms go around my neck, and I kiss her, putting every emotion I have into our lips meshing together. How did I fuck this up so badly? I'm not sure, but I know I'm going to fix it.

When a table from across the room starts whistling, I know I've taken it too far, so I pull back, smiling. "You okay?"

She laughs. "You lay that kiss on me and then ask if I'm okay?" She curls her hand into the shirt on my chest. "Yeah, I'm good. I'm better than good."

I get off my knee and make my way back to my seat. "So eat up. We need to get to the book fair before it closes."

She nods, and when she reaches for the apple fritter and takes a big bite, I know for the first time in a long time that I've done something right.

Chapter 10

Natalie

I'm standing in the aisle at the book fair, and to anyone else, I look as if I'm enthralled by the shelf of books in front of me. However, they are all a blur because I'm not thinking about books right now. No, I'm thinking about my husband and the fact that he told me he loved me in a room full of people. I shouldn't be surprised, but I am. He never, I mean ever, publicly displays affection, so the fact that he did has me second-guessing everything.

"Do you see any you like?"

Beau's voice is deep, and he's standing right over my shoulder. I act as if I've been debating on which book to look at and grab the first one I touch. My face is red when I pull the book out and look at the cover.

The shirtless man has his hand around the neck of an almost naked woman. I've read the book before and loved it. Heck, I love all this author's books, but I usually read them on my Kindle to keep the cover to myself.

Beau clears his throat, and without looking at him, I know he's pushing his glasses up his nose. I try to be quick and put the book away, but he covers my hand with his. "Wait."

His breath is hot on my neck, and I close my eyes, wishing the ground would open up and swallow me whole. He pulls the book back out of the stack and holds it up in front of me. He moves his body so that my back is pressed to his front. He lifts his other arm and encircles me in his arms with the book still held out in front of us. His voice has deepened. "What do you think this book is about?"

"Fantasies... she has fantasies, and she wants him to fulfill them."

His hips lift, and I feel his growing bulge pressed into my backside. "What kind of fantasies?"

I close my eyes, debating on answering.

When his lips press against my bare neck, I whisper to him, "They're married, and they act as if they've never met before. He picks her up in the bar of a hotel and they uh, make love."

"Hmmmm," he says while his hand that's not holding the book presses against my belly. "That's quite a fantasy. I guess you've read this book?"

I nod my head because I don't quite trust my voice.

He rubs the stubble of his chin across my neck, and it sends goosebumps across my arms. "And is that a fantasy you've had?"

I lift my shoulders, and he turns me in his arms so I have no choice but to look at him. He's bending down, searching my eyes. "Tell me, Nat. Have you thought about that? Would you like for me to pick you up at a hotel bar? We could act like we don't know each other, and I can convince you that spending the night in my arms is where you're meant to be."

I take a deep, shuddering breath. The way he describes it has me shifting my thighs together. There's a tug in my lower belly as I imagine the scenario. I've never seen this side of Beau, and I've never felt comfortable talking to him about my fantasies before. I lean my head against his chest instead of answering, and he groans in my ear. "You like that, don't you, Nat?"

My voice is muffled. "Yeah, I've had that fantasy."

He kisses me lightly on the ear, and I swear I feel his teeth dig into my sensitive flesh. "I can't wait to read it."

I pull back to look at him. "You're buying it?"

He tightens his hold on the book. "Hell, yeah, I'm buying it. I want to read all about this fantasy you've had."

He grabs my hand and pulls me in front of him. "Come on, wife. You're going to have to stay in front of me or else the whole town is going to know I have a hard-on at the book fair."

I can't help it. I giggle. Beau Blaze, the CFO of Blaze Whiskey. The man that loves spreadsheets, watching documentaries, and reading textbooks has a hard-on in the middle of town at a book fair.

He smiles as I laugh even louder. "You think it's funny, do you?"

I nod as we make it to the front. I reach for the book, thinking I'll save him from embarrassment if I buy the book instead, but he doesn't give it to me. Instead, he lays it on the makeshift counter. The older woman looks at the book and then at Beau and me. "I've read this one. Good choice."

Beau doesn't blush or seem fazed at all. "I'm looking forward to it."

He pays, and when she offers him a bag, he refuses. "It's okay. Save your bag. I'll carry it."

We are walking through town, hand in hand, and I can't seem to wipe my smile off my face.

"What are you smiling about?"

I skip a little to catch up with his long stride. "Oh nothing, just hoping we run into one of your brothers. I would love for them to see you carrying that book."

He shrugs as if it's no big deal. "You think I care? If this book gets me into your good graces, I'll carry it with the cover taped to my forehead for all I care. What anyone else thinks doesn't matter, Nat. You're all that matters."

We stop outside my gym, and I look up at him. "You mean that, don't you?"

He doesn't hesitate. "Hell yeah, I mean that."

I take a deep breath. I've been thinking about things since last night, and even though I know it's the right thing to do, I've held back. But right now, I don't want to hold back any longer. "I've been thinking..."

He nods his head but doesn't pressure me to finish. That's one of my favorite things about Beau. He has to be the most patient man I've ever known. I put my hands at his waist. "I think you should move back into the house."

I thought he'd be happy, but he frowns instead.

I pull my hands from his and hold them together in front of me. "I mean, it was just an idea. You don't have to."

He takes a step toward me. "Nat, baby, you have to know that there's no way I can lie next to you and not want to be inside you."

I roll my eyes. "I mean, duh. Ditto."

He grips my arms until it's almost painful. "You made me promise no sex."

I think about our talk the other night, and I remember exactly what was said. "Actually, we agreed no sex... unless I asked you for it."

His fingers dig into my arms, and he pulls me to him. "Are you saying...?" He takes a deep breath and asks me. "Are you asking me for sex, Nat?"

I nod. "Yeah... I mean, I think if we're going to give this our all for the next 29 days, we need to be all in... plus, I miss you. I'm not sleeping."

He looks up and down the street. "Do you have to work? Any classes left to teach today?"

I shake my head side to side. "Nope, no more classes. And Chloe is closing for me tonight."

I barely get the words out and he's bent over, his shoulder in my stomach, lifting me off the ground. When he stands up, I'm hanging over his shoulder upside down, and he starts to walk to the parking lot. "Beau, put me down. I'm too heavy."

As soon as I say it, I know I've said the wrong thing. His hand collides with my ass in a hard swat. I'm about to complain, but instead of him swatting me again, he kneads my ass cheek with his hand while he admonishes me. "It sounds to me like you need to be punished, Mrs. Blaze. I don't like hearing you talk about yourself like that."

I clench my eyes shut, and my hands tighten on his waist. "Yeah, that's another fantasy I've had."

He stops walking, and I swear I can feel his whole body tremble underneath me. Without a word, he starts walking again, and he doesn't stop until he's standing next to his SUV. He sets me on his feet, and when I'm upright, I look into his eyes. His mouth is pulled taut, almost as if he's grinding his teeth together.

He opens the car door and grunts. "Get in."

I point across the lot where mine is parked. "My car—"

He cuts me off. "Get in, Nat."

The tone of his voice has me scrambling to get into the car. I'm not scared of him in the least, but there's something in the way he demands it that doesn't leave room for any questions.

As soon as I'm seated, I don't even have time to grab the seatbelt before he's reaching in and pulling it across my chest and snapping it in place.

He slams my door and makes his way around to the driver's seat.

He pulls out of the gravel lot with a spin of his tires.

I grab on to the dash. "Beau, slow down. Are you okay? What's going on?"

"Everything's perfect. I'm going home to make love to my wife."

My heart starts to race, and I don't say another word about how fast he drives to get across town because I can't wait to make love to my husband.

Chapter 11

Beau

Natalie's quiet the rest of the way home. I take a peek at her when I'm on the straightaway, and I see her almost panting just sitting beside me. She's not alone, though, because I am doing everything I can to stop myself from speeding.

When we get to the house, I pull into the driveway and hit the garage opener. It seems it takes twice as long as normal to open before I can drive in. The anticipation is killing me.

I barely get the SUV parked and I'm out of the car, racing to the passenger side. Nat already has the door open, and I grab her around the waist and lift her out. I release her because if I'm not careful, I'll take her right here on the cold, hard garage floor.

I point to the door. "Inside."

She rears back, surprised, but does as I ask. I follow behind her, watching the way her hips shimmy back and forth with each step she takes. When we're inside, she slips her shoes off, kicking them to the side, and she starts toward the stairs probably to go to our room, but I grab on to her hand. "Where are you going?"

She points to the ceiling. "Up to the bedroom."

I shake my head. "Nope, I want you here."

She looks around the landing. "Here?"

I nod and gesture to the living room. "On the couch."

She puts her hands on her hips. "You want to make love on the couch?"

She's surprised, and I don't blame her. We've always had sex in the bedroom, behind closed doors, and I don't know why I want it any different. To me, our sex life was perfect, but after hearing about her fantasy, I'm wondering if I need to change things up. Fuck, I don't care where I have her, as long as she's mine.

I grab her hand and pull her behind me. "Oh, we're going to do more than make love, Nat. By the time this is over, I'm going to own this body. You'll never hide from me again. You'll never consider keeping it from me."

She gulps and stares up at me with wide eyes. I rub my palms down my thighs to stop from reaching for her. "Undress."

I walk around the living room that has floor-to-ceiling windows. When I reach the control panel, I hit the button, and the blinds all start to descend.

When I turn back to her, she's still standing in the same place with her clothes still on.

I walk toward her, slowly, like a predator hunting his prey. I trail one finger down her cheek. "You still have your clothes on."

The look she gives me tells me she's feeling insecure. "Let's go up to the bedroom."

I know why she wants to go to the bedroom. She wants to be able to hide from me under the covers. I've done nothing to show her how much I appreciate her body in the past, but that all changes now. From this moment on, she'll never question how much I love her body.

"Let's do it here."

She takes a breath, and for just a minute, I think she's going to fight me on it, but she grabs the hem of her shirt and pulls it over her head. The sports bra she has on underneath is the next to go. I stand in front of her with my arms crossed over my chest to stop myself from reaching for her. I'm enjoying the strip tease, and I'm going to let her finish.

She puts her hand on each side of her pants, but she doesn't lower them. "What about you? You going to undress?"

I shake my head.

"No? What do you mean no? I'm not going to be naked by myself out here."

My arms tighten around myself. I'm ready to have my hands on her but not yet. "See, the problem is, if I get naked, I won't last. I'll want to be inside you, and I want to take my time, Natalie. Plus, I need to give you your punishment."

"Punishment? For what?"

I chuckle and run my hand across the stubble of my chin. "Where should I start? Oh yeah, how about when you said you were too heavy. Let's start there."

She crosses her arms over her ample chest, hiding her berry-colored nipples from me. "I am too heavy to be carried around."

I take a step toward her and grab her hands, pulling them away from her body. I devour her with a look. While holding on to her hands, I ask her, "You removing your pants, or am I? Either way, they're coming off."

She juts her chin at me. "I'm not taking them off."

I just laugh. I walk around to the front of the couch and sit down. "Come here."

She follows me, and when she gets within reach, I grab her hips, pulling her until she's standing between my legs. With a hand on each side of her waistband, I peel her pants and panties down her legs. Her hands go to my shoulders to steady herself. "Lift your leg, baby."

She lifts her leg, and I pull the material down her thigh. I tap on her other leg and do the same. Only when she's standing in front of me completely naked do I lean back on the couch and look at her. My hands are itching to touch her, but there's something I need to do first. Pointing to my lap, I tell her, "Lie down."

Her forehead creases, and she tries to cover her body with her arms. She goes so far as crossing her legs as if that's going to keep anything from me. "What do you mean lie down?"

I hold my hand out to her. She looks at it and back to me before putting her hand gently in mine. As soon as our fingers touch, I wrap a hand around her and pull her until she falls into my lap and guide her so she's lying with her stomach on my legs and her ass in the air. She squeals and looks at me over her shoulder. "Beau, what are you doing?"

I should explain, but I know she'll figure it out. She's a smart woman. I run one hand down her back in a soft caress. Her body trembles, and when I get to her lower back, she lifts her ass up. I grab a handful of it, kneading it with my fingers as her moans fill the room. I move to the other cheek, caressing her until her body starts to go limp on my lap.

I start with a soft pat on her bottom and then the next one a little harder. She turns her head to look at me. The blue of her eyes is no longer the color of a summer sky. Instead, they are a dark blue, reminding me of nighttime. There's no denying the desire that is shining out of their depths. With her eyes on mine, I slap her ass again, and this time she whimpers, biting on to her lower lip.

I soothe my hand across her skin. "Do you like that, Nat?"

She doesn't answer me, but her eyes dilate, telling me what I already know. After another swat to her ass, I slide my hand between her thighs and cup her sex. Her body jerks as I rub my fingertips along her swollen nub. She's soaked, and she gets even wetter as I circle her clit with my fingers. "You don't have to answer me. I know you like it. Your pussy is weeping for my touch, Nat. This was meant to be a punishment. I don't want you to ever think for a second you're too heavy for me. I don't want you to think you're anything less than perfect for me."

With each word I say, I increase the pressure of my touch. With one hand, I'm caressing her back, her hips, her cheeks. With the other, I slide through her swollen slit and press a finger to her hole. She clenches on to me, and I pummel in and out of her.

"Fuck, Nat. How can you think you're anything less than exactly what I need?"

"Please, Beau. I need you. Please don't make me wait."

With a final slap to her ass and another soothing caress, I help her sit up. She straddles my lap, looping her arms around my neck. I brush her hair off her face and look at her, wondering how I got so lucky. Nat is everything to me, and I'm a fool that I almost let her walk away.

I grab on to her chin, forcing her eyes on me. "You won't leave me without a fight, Natalie. When all is said and done, you're mine, and I can't let you go."

She reaches for my shirt and pulls it up my chest. "You have too many clothes on, Beau."

I lean forward so she can remove it, and when I lean back, her hands are everywhere. She's giving me that same wide-eyed look she gave me the first time she looked at me without my shirt. She doesn't try to hide her fascination with me at all. Instead, she devours me with her eyes and touches every bare inch of me she can reach. When her hands go to the waistband of my jeans, I lean back as she unbuttons and unzips me.

"Lift up," she orders me.

I lift my thighs, taking her with me, and she laughs as she struggles to pull down my pants and underwear.

She gets them to my thighs, and I sit back down.

My cock is hard between us, and she wraps her hand around my girth. "Nat..." I groan.

She smiles as she grips me harder, and her strokes become firmer. With her hand on me, she leans forward and kisses me. Our tongues mate, and we're both breathless when she pulls back. "I need you inside me, Beau."

At that exact moment, precum oozes from my cock. I grip it tightly and put my other hand on her hip. "I want that too."

She lifts up until she's positioned her core over me and slowly starts to impale herself on my pulsating rod. She's slow about it, dragging out the movement as she clenches around me. "Fuuucckk," I moan as she lifts up and slams her body back down on mine. In our whole marriage, this is the first time I've felt her bare wrapped around me, and it's better than I ever dreamed. She's like a fitted custom-made glove that's just for me. Her pussy hugs me like she never wants to let me go.

She bounces on my lap, and her breasts sway in front of me. It's too much, and my hands dig into her hips, pulling her down onto me every time she starts to lift up. Over and over, I thrust into her. Her head falls back as I kiss her shoulder, her breasts, and every inch of skin I can reach with my mouth. Her arms wrap around my neck, and I hold her close as she grinds her pussy on me. My voice is a guttural groan. "Come, Nat. Come for me, baby."

She grinds once, twice, and then she loses all control of her body. Every muscle is pulled tight as she contracts around me. I have no choice but to follow her. I hold her waist tightly as I thrust up into her, painting her insides. My eyes roll into the back of my head because it feels so damn good.

We both collapse, panting and weak. Her head is on my shoulder, and I have to push the mass of blond hair off her face to kiss her. "I love you, Natalie."

She smiles that smile that she saves for me. "I love you too, Beau."

We lie here trying to catch our breath, and I notice when she tautens in my arms. Before I can ask her about it, she's climbing off me and gathering her clothes. "Where are you going?"

She doesn't look at me. "I need to go get cleaned up."

I nod as I look at my now semi-flaccid dick that is coated in both of our juices. "Me too. You want to shower together?"

She seems surprised but nods her head. "Uh, sure, we can do that."

I stand up and stretch my arms over my head. She's looking at me, and I know there's something on her mind. When I grab my clothes, I walk over to her. "Shower. We can talk in the shower."

She slams her mouth shut and turns to go. I follow behind her, wondering how she could ever doubt how much I want her. Already my cock is aching, wanting to be inside her again.

Chapter 12

Natalie

"All right, tell me what's on your mind."

I turn away from him to stand under the spray of the water. I let it hit me right in the face, and when I come up for air, he's moved around to the side to look at me. We've been in here for at least twenty minutes. He's washed my hair and my body, and I returned the favor. His manhood is hard between us, but he's ignoring it, and so I try to do the same. "Talk to me, Nat. What's going on in that pretty head of yours?"

I wish I could just leave it alone, but my conscience will kill me if I don't say anything. "We, uh, didn't use a condom. I mean, I'm on the pill and I take it religiously, but yeah, we didn't use a condom."

He smiles. "Trust me. I know we didn't. We'll probably never use one again. Not now that I've felt you bare. There's no going back."

He kisses me and then opens the door to the shower and reaches for a towel. Stunned, I wring out my hair and then follow him, grabbing a towel. I barely get it wrapped around me and I've followed him into the bedroom. "Wait, I don't understand. Since the very first time, you insisted you were going to wear a condom—even knowing I was on the pill—because you didn't want a child."

He shakes his head as he takes the towel to dry off his body. He frowns at me. "I never said I don't want a child."

I sputter, unable to hold back, "Uh, yes you did, which is why even though I am on the pill, you still insisted on wearing a condom... because you didn't want kids."

He shakes his head again. "I never said I didn't want kids... I needed to be sure, that's all."

My mouth drops, and I tighten the towel around me. "You needed to be sure? What does that even mean?

You didn't know if you wanted to have kids with me? Is that it?"

He walks back into the bathroom but raises his voice so I can hear him as he leaves the room. "Of course not, Nat. You're the only one I'd want to have kids with."

I walk into the closet and grab a pair of leggings and a shirt. Stalking back into the bedroom, I'm trying not to fume as I pull my drawer open to dig out my underwear and bra. I get dressed in jerky movements, and the more I think about it, the more pissed I get.

He finally comes into the bedroom, and the satisfied, relaxed smile on his face has me about to come unglued. As soon as he looks me in the face, his smile drops. "What is it? What's wrong?"

I have the towel in my hands, and unable to stand still, I use it to dry my wet hair. "What's wrong? Oh, I don't know. I just found out that my husband uses a condom when we have sex because he isn't 'sure' about me." I hold my fingers up in air quotes as I say *sure* with a snarky tone. *Not sure? What the hell does that even mean?*

He comes over and wraps his hands around my wrist. "I didn't say I wasn't sure about you... I said I wasn't sure. I know I haven't been right with you, Nat. I've already said that. But I also told you that I'm going to do better."

I'm doing my best not to cry. I don't know why it upsets me so much, but it does. "If we're going to get through this, we have to come clean. You can't drop a bomb on me like this and then not tell me what it means."

He opens his mouth and then closes it again. Never in all the time I've known him have I ever seen him completely speechless. He looks at me, unsure. As if what he's about to say is going to cause me to run or something. Oh dear God, what is it?

I shouldn't feel any sympathy for him, not with how upset I am, but I can't help but feel sympathetic to the vulnerability in his face. "Beau, talk to me."

He loosens his hold on my wrists and turns away from me. My heart drops in my chest, and it feels as if the weight of the world is on my shoulders. I expect him to walk away. That's what he's done in the past when I've confronted him about things, but he surprises me when he moves to the side of the bed and sits down.

The muscles in his chest and arms flex as he takes a deep breath and lets it out. When he finally raises his eyes and looks at me, I see the conflict in them. He pats the bed beside him. "Come here and sit down."

I put one foot out and then stop. I don't know why, but I'm scared. I've always felt that Beau has held back with me, and I've often wondered if there are things I don't know about him. Could finding out what it is make me feel different about him? But just as soon as that thought surfaces, I push it down. I force my feet to carry me across the room and sit down next to him.

He turns his body to the side, drawing one leg up on the bed so he can face me. I do the same, and once settled, he just stares at me. I can tell he's trying to form the words, and I sit here patiently, half scared and half relieved that maybe, just maybe I'm going to have more insight into our relationship.

He reaches over and puts his hand on my thigh. His fingers dig into my skin, but I don't dare move. "You're not going to like this, Natalie."

My stomach drops, and everything imaginable starts to form in my mind, but before I can put voice to any of the thoughts, he's rushing on. "When I met you, I knew that I needed you in my life. You were so much younger than me, so much more than I deserved, and we were probably doomed from the start, but I knew I had to have you. Everything happened so fast, but I didn't care. I had to have my ring on your finger."

He reaches over and rubs his finger along the band of my ring. I take in a deep breath and let it out roughly. "Okay, well, it doesn't sound bad so far. But I mean, yeah, I'm younger than you, but I'm not more than you deserve, Beau. You're a good man—"

He cuts me off with a shake of his head. "Give it up, Nat. There's nothing you or anyone can say that will convince me you can't do better than me. I know you can, but even knowing that, I can't let you go."

I cover his hand that's on my thigh with my own hand. "I don't want you to let me go."

He smiles, but it doesn't quite reach his eyes. "When we got married, even though I was fully committed, I still had my doubts. There are things about my past that you don't know about. Things I don't normally talk about."

I take in a breath and let it out, trying to prepare myself for what's to come.

He shoves one hand through his hair and then covers our hands with his free one. "I didn't have complete faith in you, Nat. In us."

My mouth drops because I wasn't prepared for that. "In me?"

He nods almost regretfully. "Yeah. You see, in my experience, women leave. They don't stay around for things."

I want to pull away from him, and I want to be mad, but I try to contain my feelings. I need to understand. "What do you mean *things*?"

"Love, marriage, babies."

I almost feel defeated. "So you married me but you thought I'd leave you?"

He looks at me through hooded eyes. There's shame on his face as he nods his head. "Yeah, which is why I wasn't surprised when you said you wanted a divorce. I knew eventually you would leave."

I open my mouth and then close it again. Is he serious right now? "Beau, look—"

He tightens his hold on me. "When I say I wasn't sure, it's because I knew I couldn't bring a baby into this world... and risk it being abandoned."

I jerk out of his hold. "You thought if I had a kid, one day I'd just leave it... leave you?"

He jams his hand through his hair. "Fuck... I know it's fucked up, Nat. In reality, I know you would never leave a child that was yours... I know that... but I'm so fucked in the head that I thought... I thought, fuck, what if you're like my mother?"

I stand up and pace back and forth across the room. All this time, I thought we were mostly happy, and come to find out, he thought I already had one foot out the door. Hell, he was never all in. He always kept me at a distance with him, his family, his business, everything. And just like that, it all makes sense. Like a light bulb has come on, I bring my hand up to my mouth with a gasp. I whirl on my foot and look at him accusingly. "Wait, is that what this is, Beau? Is this why I always felt like you had your guard up around me? Why you kept me as an outsider with your family, why you kept your distance... You expected me to leave?"

He blinks twice and nods his head. "I need to get it all out. I need to explain, Nat. When I was just a kid, our mom left us."

I rear back. All this time, he never wanted to talk about her. I assumed she'd died when they were younger. "She left you?"

He nods. "Yeah, the day she had Lucas. She left the hospital and never came back. She decided she didn't want to be a mom anymore. A husband and five boys, and she just walked out the door."

He suddenly stands up and walks across the room, pushing the curtain back to look out over the backyard. He's quiet, and I fight the urge to go to him. I take my seat back on the bed and wait. When he starts to talk again, his voice is pained. "I honestly didn't think it affected me any because years later my dad remarried, and my stepmom Charlotte was great. We made the best of it. Growing up, I never really dated women." He leans his head down and shakes it. "I'm not proud of it, but I used women for my needs and not much else. When I was in college, I met a girl. Was I in love? No, now I can say I wasn't, but we were a good fit, and we got engaged. But she broke it off after telling me that she couldn't be with me since I was emotionally inept. She felt like she couldn't get close to me, and I know that part of our relationship was true."

Fuck, another shock to the system. I murmur, "I didn't know you were engaged before."

He nods. "Yeah, it was a long time ago, and since that time, I was determined to not be serious with anyone. I knew there was a part of me that was broken. I was content with my life... until I met you. From that moment, I knew my life would never be the same. I didn't want it to be. I wanted to be with you, and I thought I could be different. I tried to be different."

I wrap my arms around myself protectively. "I don't know what to think anymore, Beau. I love you. I was all in, and now I find out you thought this was what? A temporary fling? That you planned for it to end?"

He hangs his head, unable to even look me in the eye. "No, Nat. It's not like that. I love you. Fuck, I love you so much. I thought that if I kept my distance and kept you away from my family that when you eventually left me, I would have been protecting me... protecting them. Damn, I was so wrong. So completely wrong."

He turns from the window and wipes the moisture from his cheek. "I was a fool, I know that. Hell, look at me. I'm a fuckin' mess, and I have been since you asked me for a divorce." He drops to the carpeted floor in front of me and puts his hands on both my hips. "I know I fucked up, but I can fix this. Please don't give up on me. I can't lose you, Natalie." He buries his head in my lap as his shoulders shake and his voice shudders. "I can't lose you."

I'm not sure what I'm feeling right now, but I know I've never seen this side of him before. In our whole marriage, I've never seen him vulnerable. I lift my hand off the bed and put it on the top of his head, threading my fingers through his hair. I try to soothe him, but the whole time I'm wondering *What do I do now?* My marriage has been a farce, and I don't know if we can come back from this.

Chapter 13

Beau

For three days, I worry that I've completely lost her. She's been distant and quiet, and it feels like she has put up a wall between the two of us. She asked me to move back in the other day, but after my confession on how I thought our marriage was doomed from the beginning, well, I've remained in the pool house. I've had plenty of time to myself, and I've spent most of it reflecting on our marriage and all the things I need to do differently. The other time, I spent reading the book that I picked up at the book fair. That's been eye-opening for sure. I know I need to do something. Our time for working on our relationship is running out.

I walk into her gym, but instead of wearing my workout clothes, I'm in jeans and a T-shirt. Her office door is open, and I knock on it before walking in and putting my hands in my pockets. "Hey."

She lifts her head and doesn't seem surprised. She must have seen me walk in the front door from the cameras in her office. She has a forced smile on her face. "Hey, Beau."

I cross my arms over my chest. "I have a favor to ask."

Instantly, she tenses. I know I'm not in any place to ask her for a favor, but I have an ulterior motive. I promised her I was going to do better, and I know one of the things I need to do is get her involved in my family. I point to the chair across from her desk. "Can I sit?"

She slowly nods her head.

I take a seat across from her and try not to think about the last time I was in here and how I made her come on my fingers. I pull at my jeans that seem to be getting tighter and get to the point. "Actually, my brothers and I have a favor."

She sits up a little higher, intrigued. "Your brothers?"

I nod as I rub the scruff on my chin. "Yeah, you see, it has spread everyone a little thin since I took a month off and—"

She holds her hand up and rolls her eyes. "Go back to work, Beau. You don't need a favor from me. Just do it. I mean, obviously this isn't working out, so—"

I lean forward and slap my hand on the desk. "Listen to me. I took a month off, and that's what I'm doing. Blaze needs help, but if you and I can't work on it together, then I'll just tell them no. And don't say this isn't working out because you and me not working out is not an option, so you can just take that off the table."

She looks at me with impatience. "Fine. What's the favor?"

"Blaze Whiskey is hosting a fundraiser for the new veteran facility that's opening up at the edge of town."

She leans back in her seat and crosses her arms over her chest. I try to ignore how it pushes her breasts up at the opening of her shirt. I clear my throat and force my eyes to hers before I continue. "So everything was planned, but—"

She nods her head. "But?"

"The catering and the entertainment fell through. Elle and Hudson are filling in for me since I'm gone. Lilian is assisting Ford and Lucas, so she's already spread thin. Issi, well you know Issi's going to have the baby any day, so Ford asked if there would be any way you and I could work on this together." I hold my hands up. "I know you have the gym to take care of, so if you don't have time or just can't, I understand."

Her head is tilted to the side, and I imagine her brain is going a hundred miles a minute. "When is the fundraiser?"

"Friday night."

Her eyes widen in surprise. "In three days?"

I wince, knowing that I'm pressing my luck. "Yes."

There's no hiding the hurt on her face. "And I guess that was just another function that you were going to go to without me?" She holds her hand up. "Yeah, yeah, I know the drill. I'd be bored. You would have to work the whole time, it wouldn't be any fun for me."

She throws out all the excuses I've given her in the past, and every day, I learn more and more about how ridiculous I've been. How could I have been such a fool?

I stand up and move around to her side of the desk. I lean on the edge of it and look at her. "Can you ever forgive me, Nat?"

I wait for her to tell me no and to get the fuck out of here. Hell, I'm waiting on her to pull the divorce papers from her desk drawer and insist I sign them. I know I've fucked up, but I have to fix this. When she doesn't answer me, I lean down a little and put my hand on her chin, forcing her to look at me. "I'm all in, Nat. I'll apologize to you a thousand times, hell a million if that's what it takes, but if you give me a chance, I'll show you that I'm all in. That's all I'm asking. Even though I know I don't deserve it, I'm asking you to give me another chance. Let me show you how good it can be between us."

She gently pulls from my grasp. "I'll help with the fundraiser."

Even though I know how important the fundraiser is, I don't care about it right now. "And us? What about us?"

She shrugs her shoulders. "I don't go back on my word, Beau. I said I'd give you a month." She pulls out a notepad and pencil. "All right, let's talk about the fundraiser."

I grab my eyeglasses from my pocket and put them on and hold my phone up to read the text messages from Ford. "So it's being held at the convention center in Jasper. The catering and the entertainment has canceled."

She points to my phone. "I guess you have a proposed head count and a budget?"

I ramble off the numbers, and she writes them down.

She taps her pencil on the desk. "Who was the entertainment?"

My forehead creases. "Clyde Mack."

She doesn't contain her surprise. "The up-and-coming country star? He has a new single out on the charts. *That* Clyde Mack?"

I will not be jealous that she seems to be fangirling over some country star. At least that's what I tell myself. "That's the one. Honestly, I don't see the appeal unless you're into some twenty-year-old that sings about beer, women, and his dog. From what I've seen, I don't think he owns a shirt."

She's smirking at me. Obviously, I didn't hide my jealousy too well.

"Huh, I guess I can see how that could appeal to some. I'm more into a guy that wears glasses and is into budgets and spreadsheets but still looks good with his shirt off."

My smile is instant, and because I can't hold back anymore, I pull her up from the chair she's in. I sit down and then pull her onto my lap.

She's laughing as she smacks me on the chest. "Really? We have work to do. A lot of it, actually."

I nuzzle my nose into her neck. "Nat, all this time I've wanted to hold you and have my hands on you, I've held myself back. I hope you don't mind public displays of affection because from this point on, if I want to hold your hand, touch you, kiss you... I'm going to do it."

She pants out a breath. "I don't mind it. Actually, I think I like it."

I put my hand to her cheek and bring her lips to mine. I put everything into the kiss. All my insecurities, my fear, my love, all of it. She's pressed up against me, our bodies flush to one another, and she's the one to break contact. Her lips are swollen and her nose red. Her eyes are that dark shade of blue that tells me she wants more, but her hand on my chest stops me from reaching in again. "We have work to do, Beau."

I take deep breaths, and when I've calmed down, I nod my head. "Of course, you're right. So the details for the event..." I shift in my seat because her hip is pressed up against my hard manhood, and it sucks to ignore it, but just being this close and having her in my arms is enough right now. "We are charging $100 a ticket. The food was hors d'oeuvres and desserts. You already know what the entertainment was."

She nods. "Okay, I need to make some calls."

I hand her my phone, but she doesn't take it. "I can use mine."

I shrug and push mine into her hand. "Take mine. Yours is out of reach, and I don't want you to get up."

She takes my phone and holds it between both her hands. She looks at the blank screen and then hands it to me. "You need to put your passcode in it."

I don't take the phone. "It's your birthday."

Her jaw slacks. "Your passcode is my birthday?"

She's typing in the code when I answer her. "Yes, and your picture is my screen saver."

At that moment, a picture of Nat pops up on my screen. Her eyes go to mine, and I can see the surprise on her face, reminding me yet again of what a fool I've been.

I lean back in my chair as she works. She calls Chloe to see if she can cover the next three days at the gym.

After that, she calls Sugar Glaze Bakery and talks to Emery, the owner. After some back and forth, they come up with a dessert menu, and Emery is able to cater desserts for Friday night.

She then calls Violet, the owner of Red's Diner, and in less than ten minutes, she has the food situation completely covered.

When she hangs up, I can't help but be impressed. "Did you really just take care of the catering in less than twenty minutes?"

She shrugs. "And people will love the food. You know it's good. I'm not sure why you all didn't go with them anyway. They do a lot of catering in Whiskey Run."

"I'm not sure, but we'll be sure to spread the word if they do a great job. Okay, entertainment..."

She tries to get up, but I wrap my arms around her waist. She smiles, kisses my nose, and puts her hands on my shoulders. "I think better if I pace."

I growl. I don't mean to, but I do. I'm about to let her up, but instead she settles back into my lap and against my chest. "Okay, fine. I'll think here."

I hold her in my arms and don't say a word. I would let her think like this all day if I could. I'm staring at her when she opens her eyes. She sits up a little bit but doesn't try to get up. "You're looking at me differently, Beau. I'm not sure what to make of it."

I twirl a piece of hair that has come out of her ponytail around my finger. "I probably am looking at you differently. I feel different."

I feel her tense, but she tries to hide it. "What do you mean you feel different?"

"I dunno how to explain it, and I don't want to screw this up again. It's probably better if we don't talk about it."

She leans into me and presses her chest against mine. She's fighting dirty. "We need to talk about it. Try and explain it to me."

I let out a ragged breath. "I don't know. I feel like I always held myself back. The things I thought, wanted, craved... I held it all back. And now, after realizing that there's a chance I can lose you, I can't hold it back anymore. I haven't been living, Nat."

She puts her hand on my chest. I know she can feel the steady drumming of my heart. "And now you are."

I cover her hand with mine. "And now I am."

She curls into me, pressing her head against my chest. I rest my chin on the top of her head. She's not tense. She doesn't seem like she's mad; if anything, she's completely melted into me. I kiss the top of her head again and just hold her.

It's a while later before I hear her mutter the words, "I think I have an idea."

"Huh?"

She leans back to look at me. "I think I have an idea for the entertainment."

"What is it?"

She holds her hands up. "Okay, hear me out. I'm not sure we can reach the population of Clyde, but we can get butts in seats with this idea."

I nod. "Okay, I'm liking it so far because ticket sales are low."

She nods, and it's obvious she's excited. She jumps off my lap, and I reluctantly let her go. She starts to pace. "We have dance teams that practice in the studio every week. What if we do a show with them? Oooh, and the high school cheerleaders and dance team. Oh my, and the band at the high school."

I take my glasses off and pocket them in my shirt. "I don't know. You think people will pay to see that? I'm not sure, Nat."

She laughs. "Okay, how much are tickets?"

I wince. "One hundred dollars. But you get entertainment and food."

She comes over to me and squats with her hands on my thighs. "Okay, so would you pay a hundred dollars to go see Ollie play soccer if he was invited to do something like this?"

Instantly, I'm nodding my head. "Yes, of course."

She squeezes my legs. "And what about the rest of your family? They wouldn't want to miss it either, right?"

I grab her arms and pull her onto my lap. "I think you're on to something, Mrs. Blaze."

I try to kiss her, but she's pushing on my chest. "Stop, we can't. We have so much to do. We need to come up with a plan. I bet all of them already have choreography for patriotic songs, and that would be great for the facility. We could have a theme."

I interrupt her. "We do have a sound guy. We just need the music tracks."

She claps her hands together. "See, it's all working out. Okay, I'm going to call the dance coach and the high school. Can we do a rehearsal Friday morning?"

I nod. I'm not sure if it's possible, but for her, I'll pay whatever I need to pay to make sure the convention center can accommodate us. "Yes, sure. Whatever you need."

She leans into me and hugs me. "Oh, this is so fun, Beau. I promise, I won't let you down. It's going to be perfect."

She's out of my arms before I can answer her. She's walked across the room, holding up my phone. "I'm going to get calling. Oh, and can you send me ticket information so I can start selling tickets?"

I stand up and right my clothes. "Elle felt bad and said she can still work on selling tickets. I think she thought she was putting too much on us."

Nat waves her phone at me. "Tell Elle not to worry. Consider the tickets sold. The families are going to buy tickets."

I follow her, wanting to be close. "What can I do?"

"Well, I thought I'd go to the high school to meet with the band director and the cheerleading and dance coaches. Want to go with me?"

I hold my hand out to her. "Let's do it."

She looks at my hand and takes it in her own. She goes to her tiptoes and plants a kiss on me before sinking back to the heels of her feet. "Let's do it."

I walk with her through the gym. She stops to talk to Chloe for a minute, and we're soon out the door. I know I have a long way to go, but I'm going to right all my wrongs.

Chapter 14

Natalie

I double- and triple-check everything. The rehearsal this morning went off perfectly. It's amazing what we've accomplished in such a short amount of time. The woman that teaches dance at the studio came up with a whole line-up of popular songs for the night, and everything just fell into place. The dance team and cheerleaders were able to adjust a dance for their song. The band already knew the song they were assigned. It worked out perfectly.

And now, here I am standing here all alone in my brand-new dress and shoes, fidgeting.

"Aah, there you are. I've been looking for you."

I felt his presence before I heard him. I'm worried about tonight for more reasons than I can count. Of course, I'm hoping that everything works out, but probably what I'm most worried about is Beau and me. This is our first big event since he's said things are different. What if they're not different at all? What if this is another let-down and I spend the evening on my own, listening to some woman I barely know say, "I didn't know Beau Blaze was married"?

Damn, I can't take it.

Beau turns me in his arms. "Hey, what's wrong? Everything is perfect. I saw Elle, and she said the tickets are sold out. As a matter of fact, they sold some standing only tickets because they're out of seats. You did it, Nat."

I put my hands on his chest. "We did it. We're a pretty good team, Beau."

He nods his head. "We're the best team. Nat, you're beautiful." He trails his fingers over my bare shoulder. "And no matter how good you look in this dress, I think I'm going to like it better when it's lying on our bedroom floor."

My eyes widen with understanding. I know what he's asking me, but I want to hear it. "What do you mean?"

He grips my shoulders and pulls me flush against him. "I want to move back in, baby. I want to go to sleep and wake up with you in my arms."

I want to say yes. Everything inside me wants to say yes.

People are pouring in, and I know we can't keep standing off to the side. He has duties. As the CFO of Blaze, I know he'll be donating a check later tonight. I pull at the lapel of his jacket and point to where his brothers are all standing with their wives and fiancées. "You'd better get to it, Mr. Blaze."

I take a step back and am about to go in the opposite direction. I know I can check on the food and the desserts, but I'm sure Emery and Violet have it completely under control. But I could probably hang with them in the kitchen or even help carry things out. I've never been one for just standing by. I take two steps before I feel Beau moving behind me. He loops his hand into mine, and I stop. "What are you doing?"

He looks in front of us. "I don't know. What are we doing?"

I force a smile to my face. "You're going out there and doing your thing. I'm going to make sure everything is ready."

He just smiles at me. "Everything is ready. And I'm doing my thing."

I try to pull my hand from his, and he threads our fingers together and holds my hand tighter. I pull our hands up. "Okay, what exactly is your thing? Because I don't think you're going to get anything done like this."

He holds our hands up to his chest. "This is my thing, Nat. Whatever you're doing, I'm doing. I want to spend the evening with my wife. Is that so bad?"

I shake my head slowly. "No, but..."

He smiles at me. "No buts. Now do you really need to go check on things, or can we go over to where our family is waiting on us?"

I stutter out the words. "Our family?"

He nods and points to where all his brothers and their families are standing. "Yeah, our family."

There's a yearning inside me. I want to go over there with him, but fear is holding me back. "Uh, you go ahead. I'll be there in a while."

His smile drops, but he doesn't let me go. "Don't do this, Nat. Don't draw into yourself. Don't think about the past. Think about now and our future. I want to take you over there to my family. I want to hear them brag on how you've saved this whole event. I want to introduce you to all the people here as my wife. I want—fuck, I can't believe I'm saying this—I want to see the men that look at you and for them to know you're going home with me. I promise you... I'm not going to let you down. I'm going to stay right by your side the whole night." He holds up a finger. "I do have to do a small speech, but I won't be gone long."

I take a shaky breath. "Are you sure about this, Beau?"

He nods and kisses my forehead, our hands still tucked against his chest. "I've never been more sure of anything in my life."

I take a deep breath. There's a part of me that knows if I go over there, I'm agreeing one hundred percent to giving us another chance. It's no longer just empty words; I'm going to play this out and give it my all. I nod my head. "Okay, let's go."

He instantly starts walking across the foyer. He's like a man on a mission, or he's afraid I'm going to change my mind or something. As soon as we get near his family, they all start talking at once.

"There she is... the woman of the hour."

"You saved us, Natalie."

"What would we have done without you?"

I'm passed around between all of them. They each take turns hugging me, but Beau never leaves my side. Ford, the oldest brother, stops me. "Thank you for everything you've done this week, Natalie. We could never have pulled this off without your help. I know you have your gym, but at some time, I'd like to talk to you about possibly helping us part-time with special events."

I look at Beau, and he's smiling proudly at me. I turn back to Ford. "Uh, sure, I'd love that."

He nods, and I get passed back to Huddy and his fiancée, Elle. Elle is hugging me. "I'm sorry to be pawing you the very first time we meet, but I have to hug you. You saved me this week. I was way over my head. I can't believe you sold all those tickets. And what a great idea with the performers. It was perfect."

Overwhelmed with everyone's kindness, all I can stutter out is "Thank you."

Huddy puts a hand on my shoulder. He hasn't been home from the military for a long time, but obviously being home has been good for him. "My brother fucked up."

My mouth drops, and I look over at Beau. The smile is gone from his face, but he doesn't look like he's mad or anything. Huddy continues, "He fucked up, but I have no doubt he loves you. Don't give up on him, okay?"

I look at the massive man in front of me. He's intimidating to most everyone, I would think. Especially me, since I have to practically lay my head backwards to look up at him. I'm pretty sure his hand could stretch all the way around my neck. But I'm not scared of him. Not in that sense. "Okay," I mutter.

"Okay, okay. I think we should take our seats. The show is starting soon."

Beau brings our hands up and kisses mine before walking with me to our seats. We take up a whole aisle with his family. I'm a little giddy as Elle moves to make sure she can sit next to me. There's small talk all around us, and I sit here and pray that everything works out, not only on stage but with everything else too.

Ford speaks first and welcomes everyone. The atmosphere is electric, and I love seeing everyone excited and happy. Ford talks about the importance of the facility and mentions how it's going to serve the wounded heroes and make a difference in so many lives. I get a little overwhelmed emotionally being a part of all this. Beau leans toward me and whispers, "You okay?"

I nod my head as I wipe a lone tear. "Yeah, I'm fine. I'm good."

"I need to go up to present the check. You want to go with me?"

Vigorously, I shake my head side to side. There's no way I'm going up there in front of all these people. "No, thank you. I'll stay right here."

He laughs quietly. "All right, I'll be right back." He kisses me before walking down the aisle and then toward the front of the auditorium.

Ford introduces a few businesses that are sponsoring tonight's events. Each of them comes forward and announces their donations. Beau is standing to the side, his eyes on me the whole time. When it's his turn, he goes to the podium and talks. "Uh, I have something planned to say, but first I wanted to thank someone special. Earlier this week, we had a bit of a hiccup with this event. In the span of a few hours, we lost our catering, and our entertainer had to cancel. I want to thank my wife, Natalie Blaze, for all the hard work she put into tonight. She recruited our caterers —Sugar Glaze Bakery for the desserts and Red's Diner for the hors d'oeuvres. And the entertainment, the performers, dancers, cheerleaders, and band— she's put together a great ensemble and I'll tell you I saw dress rehearsals earlier today, and it is amazing. Anyway, Nat, please stand up."

My mouth drops. I would sink farther into my seat if Elle wasn't sitting next to me, dragging me up to stand. I look around the huge convention center. The whole town of Whiskey Run is here. I know my face is red, and it gets even worse when everyone around us starts to clap.

When it dies down, Beau continues, "Thank you, Nat. I love you, and I don't know what I'd do without you."

I mouth the words *I love you too*. He smiles and continues his speech. He talks about how important the facility is to Blaze Whiskey as a company. He talks about his brother Huddy, who just got back from the military and how the services are going to help so many lives. He presents the check, and there's an audible gasp in the crowd when he announces the amount. He's making his way back to where I'm sitting and watching me the whole way. When he sits down, I can feel all the eyes on us. If there are people in town that didn't know Beau Blaze was married, they do now. And heck, anyone not here tonight will know tomorrow. All my insecurities are suddenly lifted. I lean into him, and he puts an arm around my shoulder. "Yes."

He puts a finger under my chin. "Yes what?"

"Yes, I want you to move back into the house... into our bedroom tonight."

His body jerks. "Are you sure, Nat?" He leans in to whisper into my ear, "Once I'm back in, I'm never leaving again. We'll work through any problems we have, but I'm not leaving you again."

I slide my hand to his thigh and squeeze. "I like the sound of that, Beau."

He covers my hand with his. "Me too."

Chapter 15

Beau

"Nat, baby?"

I spent the last two hours loving her body, trying to make up for lost time. We're both exhausted, but I can't sleep.

Her voice is tired, and I know I'm keeping her awake. "Yeah?"

"Thank you for everything you did to help with tonight. We really couldn't have done it without you."

I can hear the smile in her voice. "I'm pretty sure you just spent the last two hours thanking me."

I span my hand across her lower back, pressing her body against mine. My cock stirs. "I could probably go another round."

She's sprawled out on top of me. Her legs are wrapped around mine, and her head is resting on my chest, right on my heart. She runs a finger along my rib cage. "I think we should sleep. We have tomorrow."

I run my hand down her back and swat her softly on the ass. "You mean we have forever."

I hold my breath, waiting for her response. Waiting for her to tell me we have thirty more days or something else like that. But I breathe easier when I hear her huskily say, "Forever."

Before I can stop myself, I blurt out the question that's been on my mind. "How many children do you want to have?"

She lifts her head up and looks at me through hooded eyes, blinking. "What?"

I shrug, trying to hide my excitement. It's like a switch has been turned on inside me, and now I can't think of anything but getting her pregnant. She pats me on the chest and asks again, "What did you say,

Beau?"

I kiss her forehead. "You know exactly what I said, but if you're wanting to act like you didn't hear me, I can ask you another time."

She rests her chin on my chest. "I'm just surprised, I guess."

I stroke my hand through her soft hair. "I want a boy and a girl."

"So two kids?"

I chuckle. "Honestly, I liked having so many brothers, and if I thought I could convince you that we should have four or six kids, I would."

She raises up on her elbows. "Four or six?"

I lift my head and shift my pillow to raise my head a little. "Yeah. Definitely an even number."

She whistles softly and shakes her head. "I don't know if I could handle four or six boys."

"Oh no, not all boys. I definitely want us to have a little girl. We need to have the boys first, though, so they can look out for their little sister."

She laughs and then looks offended. "Any girl of mine is going to be able to take care of herself. She won't need her brothers or her dad—"

I cut her off as I run my hand through her hair and then down her back. "Oh, sweetie, you have no idea. Of course she's going to be able to take care of herself, but she won't have to. She'll have me and her brothers to protect her. And I already know that we'll be fighting the boys off if she looks anything like you."

It's obvious she likes my comment by the way she smiles at me. "Stop."

I wrap both arms around her and pull her closer to me. "What? It's the truth."

She rolls her eyes and leans her head back on my chest. She's quiet, and I just lie here, enjoying the feel of her pressed against me. I've told myself over and over that I'm not going to fuck this up again, and I know that the last time we talked about kids, it didn't go well, but I couldn't stop myself this time.

She is circling her finger around my nipple, stroking through the hair on my chest. "You know, we don't have to rush into anything. We can wait."

I open my mouth and then close it again. I can't see her face, and I need to see it. I want to know what she's thinking. I push her to her back and lie on top of her. I brush the hair off her face and stroke my finger along her cheek. "Are you saying that for my benefit, or is that what you want? Do you want to wait?"

Her eyes are searching mine, and she shrugs her shoulders into the bed. She tries to look away, and I stop her. "Talk to me."

The look she gives me is defiant. "Do you want the truth?"

"Of course I do."

She lifts her chin. "Fine, then, if it was up to me, we would have started having children right away. I would have had your child right after we got married, Beau. I knew when I married you that I wanted to have kids with you. I was all in."

Her words gut me. I lean my head against her belly and take a deep breath. "I'm a fool."

She cuts me off by putting her hand on my chin and bringing my face up. She covers my mouth with her hand. "Don't say that. You're not a fool. I understand more about you now than I ever did, Beau, and even though it hurts—I won't lie, it hurts—I understand why you did what you did. I can't act like I know everything you went through, but I'm here, Beau, and I'm not leaving."

I grab her hand and take it off my mouth. "I love you, Nat." I slide up her body and kiss her lips. "It's you and me now. You are what matters to me."

She slides her arms around my neck and changes the subject. "So there's something I need to tell you."

I lie down next to her and throw a leg and arm over her and pull her so I'm cocooned all around her. "Let's hear it."

"Lilian invited me to Ollie's soccer game Monday night."

I can't hold back my yawn. I'm starting to wear down now, but at least tonight I'll be able to sleep since I'll have Natalie in my arms. "Okay, sounds good. Or do you not want to go? We can do whatever you want to do."

Her voice is unsure, and I know it's because of our past and the way I made her feel. "Do you want me to go?"

I hold her tighter. "Yes, I want you to go. Anywhere and everywhere I go, I want you to be by my side."

She sighs and smiles. "Okay, we'll go together then."

I thread our fingers together and kiss her on the forehead. "Night, wife. I love you."

She burrows her naked body into mine. "I love you, too."

I've wasted so much time, and I've been given a second chance. I won't waste a second of it. From this point on, I'm doing everything I can to be exactly what Natalie needs.

Chapter 16

Natalie

"You guys, I'm not going to the sex club."

All of my friends laugh, but Jilly is the first one to answer. "Yeah, yeah, we got it. You don't want to go to the sex club. You've told us that at least ten times since we left Whiskey Run."

Chloe chimes in. "Plus, it's book club night. We have to save the sex club for another night when we're not talking books."

I turn around in my seat and look at the car full of my friends. Chloe, Jilly, Abby, and Olivia are all with me, and they are not good at hiding things. They're up to something, and by the way they're acting, I don't think I'm going to like it.

"So where are we going?"

Chloe, who's driving, looks in the rearview mirror. "Yeah, Jilly, where are we going?"

I gasp. "You're driving. You better know where we're going." I turn in my seat to look at Jilly, and she's making faces. "Jilly, where are we going?"

She scrunches up her nose. "To The Imperial."

I put my hand on the dash and turn farther in my seat. "The Imperial? The hotel in Jasper? Why would we be going to a hotel? Oh my gosh, you guys, how do I explain this to Beau? *Hey Beau, by the way I'm going to a hotel in Jasper.* I'm not sure he's going to like me hanging out in hotel restaurants."

Jilly rolls her eyes. "Call him and tell him. If he says no, we'll go somewhere else."

I pull my phone from my purse. "You guys, we're doing so well right now, I don't want to mess it up. I need to at least tell him what we're doing so he doesn't think I'm keeping anything from him."

Olivia cuts in. "Girl, are you kidding me? You don't need to ask permission."

I knew Olivia would give me shit. Ever since she caught her ex cheating, she's been fed up with all men. I try to placate her. "I'm not asking for permission, but I do know that if he was having a night out at a hotel, I'd want to know. I'm just giving him the same respect I would want from him."

I no sooner get the words out than he answers the phone. "Hey, baby."

Shit, why didn't I just stay home? Honestly, I forgot all about book club until Jilly called me this morning to remind me. Hearing the huskiness of his voice, I wish I had backed out. "Hey, so I just wanted to let you know that we're having book club at The Imperial downtown."

"Okay, baby. Have fun."

I pull the phone back from my ear and look at it before putting it back against my ear. "Uh, you don't mind?"

He laughs. "Why would I mind?"

Oh I don't know, I'm scantily dressed and going to drink at a hotel. That's what I think, but I don't say it. "No, you're right. You shouldn't. I was just letting you know."

He rushes out the rest. "All right, well, have a good night and be safe. Love you, babe."

I'm about to tell him I love him too when I hear the phone click.

I quietly put my phone back in the purse, and Jilly is the first one to speak. "See, we're good."

I nod and cross my arms over my chest. "Yep, we're good."

I'm not sure what I expected, but I did think that maybe just maybe he'd be a little more surprised or protective of me. I let the thought linger for just a minute, and then I push it aside. *Beau and I are good. We're good, and this is just a night out. I'm glad he trusts me.*

When we get to the hotel, Chloe pulls in right up front where the valet parking is. We all pile out of her car, and I tug at the too-short skirt I'm wearing. Jilly told me to dress up—heck, she showed up at my house with this outfit as a gift. How could I tell her no?

"So where is the restaurant?" I ask one of the men working the valet.

He points toward the front doors. "Through there and then down the hallway."

We walk into the lobby, and I gasp as I look around. I've never been in this hotel before, and it is amazing. I twirl on my heels, looking at the grand ceiling. Everything is in gold and black, even the extra long and wide couches that are spaced around the beautiful greenery. "Wow."

Jilly comes up to me and puts her hand on my chin. "Close your mouth."

I laugh and look around. "Do you blame me? This is nice."

She loops her arm in mine. "Yes, it is. Come on, our reservation isn't for another hour. Let's go to the bar."

"The bar?" I ask her uneasily. I don't know why I feel so weird about all this, but I do.

Chloe, Olivia, and Abby all come to a stop next to us. "Yep, the bar. Let's go."

We walk out of the lobby, and we're immediately seated at a table toward the back of the bar. We each take turns ordering, and I'm the last to go. "I'll just take a water, please."

Jilly rolls her eyes. "She'll have a Peachy Keen."

I wait for the server to walk away. "If you all are drinking, I need to stay sober. Someone has to drive."

Olivia is digging in her purse. "Nope. Not since we're staying at the hotel."

I jerk my head toward her. "What? I'm not staying here."

Jilly leans toward me. "Calm down, Nat." She starts to mumble, and I know I didn't hear her right.

I spurt out a laugh. "Did you just call me high maintenance?"

She rolls her eyes. "If the shoe fits."

I put my hands up on the table. "Look, it's no big deal. I didn't plan on staying all night. I'll just get Beau to come get me later. No biggie."

I reach for my purse to get my phone out, and Jilly grabs my hand. She gestures over my shoulder. "Uh oh, don't look now, but there's a man behind you, and he looks like he's completely checking you out."

I snort and try to pull my phone up to dial Beau. "You can have him."

Jilly grabs the phone. "I dunno if you're going to want to pass him up. He looks hot... and rich."

I shrug, and all of them are staring at me with smiles on their faces. "Like I said, you can have him."

Jilly rolls her eyes. "You at least have to check him out."

I hold my hand up with my wedding ring on it. "No, I don't. I'm happily married. I don't need to 'check him out.'"

Jilly lifts her shoulder. "Just look at him."

I shake my head. "Nope, I don't want to give him the wrong idea. I'm good, really. One of you have at it."

Olivia leans forward. "Oh God have mercy, Nat. Turn around. I'm begging you, please just turn around."

I look at all my friends, who are all staring at me with weird smiles on their face. I slowly turn in my seat and look over my shoulder... and my mouth drops. "What?"

Jilly squeezes my hand and lets go of my phone. "Go ahead, Momma Nat. We're going to dinner and staying the night at the hotel, so you won't have to worry about us. Go get your man."

Speechless, I get up from my seat and make my way across the bar. As I look at him, I can feel my heart start to race. He's in a suit and tie, and when he turns toward me, he's wearing all black from head to toe. I stop next to him and stutter, "Beau, what are you doing here? I mean, I'm glad you're here... but what's going on?"

He lifts his drink up and takes a sip. The whole time he does, he slowly lifts his eyes to my face and then gazes down the length of my body. Desire is evident on his face. When his eyes meet mine again, his voice is low and husky. "Hey, I saw you walk in. You're beautiful." He holds out his hand as if he wants me to take it. "I'm Beau Blaze."

My mouth falls open, and I finally catch on. The book... he read the book. He's got the black suit on... he's drinking from a glass of whiskey, and damn he's got the look of desire down to a T. I reach my hand out and put it in his. "I'm Natalie... I'm—"

He cuts me off when he pulls my hand until I tumble into his lap. He pulls me against him and grunts into my ear, "You're mine, Natalie Blaze."

Desire forms low in my belly, and I settle in his lap. He holds me close and kisses me until I'm breathless. With the way his tongue slides against mine and the way he strokes his hand up and down my back, I could lie down on this bar top and ask him to take me right here. He pulls back and whispers into my ear, "I thought I could do this, act as if we're strangers and convince you to come up to my hotel room, but from the moment you walked in, I've been on edge."

His hand slides to my inner thigh, where my skirt has ridden up. The pad of his finger rubs roughly across my skin, and my legs fall wider. "I wasn't thinking right when I bought this. I wanted to see you in it, but I didn't think about other men seeing you like this."

I pull back. "You bought this for me?"

He nods and puts his finger under the strap at my shoulder. "I did. I had it all planned out tonight, but I think I've ruined it."

I loop my arms around his shoulders. "So did you book a hotel room?"

He clears his throat and pulls at the collar of his shirt. "I did. I had hopes..."

I smile ear to ear. "Oh, it's happening. Let's go."

I stand up, and he's quick to follow. Before I can take a step, he grabs my hips and pulls me back against his body. His cock is hard, and his voice is gruff in my ear. "Don't go too far, or everyone in here is going to know exactly what we're leaving here to go do."

I press my ass back and am about to close my eyes when I look over at the table with all my friends. Every one of them are looking at us with their mouths hanging open. I turn in Beau's arms. "Well, it looks like we've given them a show."

Normally, something like this would embarrass him, but he doesn't seem to care. "None of that matters. I need to get you to our room, Nat."

I agree with him wholeheartedly. "Let's go."

I grab his hand and make sure that I walk out in front of him. I wave at my friends as we pass their table, and I hear them all thank him for dinner and the hotel room.

I'm searching for the elevators, and when I find them, I head straight down the hall, not stopping until I'm standing front of the big silver doors. I push the button before turning to him. "You bought my friends dinner and a hotel room?"

He nods. "Yep, I needed to thank them for getting you here."

The elevator opens, and he walks me backward into the elevator. He hits the button for the seventh floor and then pushes me flush against the wall. His leg comes up between mine and presses at my core. His mouth is at my throat, and when his tongue travels from my shoulder blade and up the side of my neck, I'm about to fall into a limp pile right here in the elevator.

The elevator dings, and he breaks away. I catch sight of myself in the mirror outside the elevator, and already I look thoroughly ravished. We walk down the hallway and stop at a door. He pulls a key card from his pocket and runs it through the lock. It takes him three tries, but finally the light turns green and he pushes the door open.

I barely get inside, and I'm pressed into the wall with Beau against my backside. His cock digs into my back, and he doesn't waste any time. He pulls at my skirt, lifting it up and baring my ass. He cups me, and his whole body trembles against me. His voice is gruff in my ear. "So help me, Nat, if you came out dressed like this tonight without any underwear on, I'm going to smack your ass."

I physically jerk. "Now you're making me wish I'd left my thong at home."

As soon as I say *thong,* he moves to the center of my ass and pulls on the string between my ass cheeks. The way he tugs, it rubs against my core, and I raise to my tiptoes. He hasn't even touched me there yet, and already I'm soaked and ready for him.

He slides his hand between my legs, pushing the material to the side before stroking his finger through my wet core. "Fuuuucckk," he groans. "You're soaked, baby. So fucking wet."

I spread my legs wider apart and push my ass out. "I've been wet since I saw you sitting at the bar, Beau."

He kisses down my neck. "I've fucked this up, Nat. I wanted it all to be perfect. I wanted to make your fantasies come true, but you're too fuckin' tempting. I have no restraint when it comes to you."

I try to concentrate on his words, but the way he's rubbing his fingers along my swollen clit has everything in my mind just a big, fuzzy mess. He pulls his hand away, and I turn in his arms and grab on to his jacket. "Don't stop. Please, don't stop."

"I'm not stopping. I need you naked."

He's pulling at my shirt, and I help him get my bra off. As fast as I can, I pull the rest of my clothes off and then reach for his jacket. "Clothes off."

He takes the jacket off, and I'm pulling at the buttons on his shirt. My hands are shaking, and I can barely get them through the holes. In frustration, I pull at his shirt, popping the rest of the buttons right off. "Sorry. I'm sorry, but I don't want to wait."

Chapter 17

Beau

I grab her hands and shove them over her head against the wall. My chest is heaving, and I use my hips and hands to hold her still. "Stop."

She glares at me. "So help me, if you stop right now, it's not going to be good for you, Beau Blaze."

I'm panting. Fuck, all I want to do is pull my cock out and enter her in one thrust, but I'm trying to take my time and do this right.

"I'm not stopping. I'm just slowing it down." I tilt my hips toward her, pressing my hard rod into her belly. "Trust me, I'm so fucking hard I'm going to blow unless we slow down."

"We can go slow another time. Please, I need you, Beau."

I lean in and kiss her, and as soon as her tongue slides into my mouth, I'm holding in a moan. I pull back. Fuck! The fantasy. She told me exactly what she wanted, and I've screwed it up. But I wasn't lying. I've been on edge all afternoon, knowing what was going to happen tonight. I'm usually more disciplined, but Nat makes me crazy. "The fantasy—"

She cuts me off as she reaches for the waistband of my pants. "You're my fantasy, Beau. You are in every fantasy I have. This right here is a fantasy. Where you want me so badly you can't hold back. That all you want is to bury yourself inside me... that's a fantasy of mine."

I croak out the word. "Bare... bury myself into you bare."

She yanks down my zipper, reaches in, and wraps her hand around my girth. "Yes. That. I want that."

She strokes my cock, and precum oozes from my tip. She tightens her grip on me, and I put my hand on her wrist to hold her still. "Beau," she moans in frustration.

"I'm not coming in your hand, Nat. You know where I want to come."

She gives me her most innocent look. "If you don't want to come in my hand, where do you want to come?"

I grab the string of her underwear, ripping the thin material. As it falls to the floor and I palm her pussy, I press into her. "Here. Right here is where I want my cum."

Her hips push out, trying to get more friction where she needs it.

When I pull my hand back, her body deflates, and she glares at me.

I push my pants and underwear down my thighs and then wrap my arms around her waist and lift her up. Her hands go to my shoulders, and I settle her right over my cock. Slowly, she comes down my shaft, and I suck in a breath as sweat covers my brow. When she's completely impaled on my rod, I thrust into her, going deeper. She grunts as her back bangs against the wall.

Over and over, I pummel my hips into her, taking her deeper and deeper. She's moaning my name over and over. I lean her back against the wall, one arm around her hips and the other reaching down between us. I barely touch her clit with my finger and her whole body jerks. Her nails dig into my shoulders, and I grunt in pain as she digs her heels into my ass, pulling me deeper.

I rest my forehead against hers. "Come for me, Nat. Come all over my dick. I want you messy and all over me. Give it to me."

Her pussy clamps down on me like a vise. She plasters herself to me as she rides the wave of the orgasm that completely takes over her body. I come, shooting my seed deep inside her. I'm grunting her name, pulling her hips, riding the last waves of the explosion.

Breathless, I lean us both against the wall, my head cradled at her breast.

"Beau."

I'm still trying to catch my breath. "Yeah?" I answer her with a puff of air.

She grabs on to my shoulders. "Put me down. You're going to break your back."

I pull back, glaring at her. "Sometimes I think you want to be punished."

I walk her slowly toward the bed. It's hard to do because my pants are around my legs. I lean her over, holding her close to me until her back hits the bed. I try to lift up, but she holds me close. "If you're talking about spanking me, then yeah, I'll take that punishment."

I lift a brow to her. "Another fantasy?"

She smiles cheekily at me. "Yep. You know I liked it last time. I love everything you do to me, husband."

The way she's looking at me has my blood pressure spiking. "I'm game. Give me five minutes. I need some water."

I stand up and remove the rest of my clothes. She leans up on her elbows, completely checking me out. "I'll give you ten. I mean, we have all night."

I lean over and kiss her. "We have forever."

The rest of the night, I give her what she wants. I've touched, kissed, licked every inch of her body, and it's not enough. It will never be enough.

Chapter 18

Natalie

My whole body is sore. I think I used muscles I didn't know I had.

It probably didn't help any that we got a late check-out and I had to hurry home and teach a class this afternoon. I'm tired. Heck, I'm way past tired, but it was all worth it.

And now here I sit at the park, about to walk in for Ollie's game, and my nerves are taking over. I wanted to be invited for so long, and now that I am, I'm second and triple guessing everything. Am I wearing the right thing, do I sit with his family, are they going to think it's weird that I'm just now coming, am I doing the right thing, should I have just gone home?

Chloe was late getting to the gym, so I told Beau to go ahead without me. I didn't think I'd be this nervous when I got here, though.

But here I am, and I'm not happy with myself. I don't like this side of me. The self-sufficient, independent woman that I usually am is gone, and it pisses me off.

I pull my shoulders back and pull down the mirror over the visor. Instead of checking my makeup or my hair, I'm looking at my eyes. I see the pain from the past still there, but I also see the hope and positive attitude that's been a part of me my whole life. I can do anything. I can take on any challenge, and making the best of this, doing what I can to save my marriage, is probably the biggest challenge of my life.

But I can do it.

With my resolve set, I put the visor back up. I turn off my car and get out, pulling the crossbody strap of my purse over my arm. Smoothing my hands down my legs, I start walking toward the soccer field.

I get to the field, and the first people I recognize are Isabella and Lucas. They're standing with their backs to me, and Lucas is rubbing Issi's back. She's due soon, and I know everyone in the family is anxiously waiting for the little one's arrival.

I stop next to Issi and put my hand at her back. When she turns, I can't help but notice her round stomach. Did it grow since last night? "Oh my gosh, Issi! You're glowing."

She grimaces, but she still insists on pulling me in for a hug. "I don't feel like I'm glowing, but thank you. The fundraiser was perfect. All the guys have been talking about how you pulled off a miracle."

I can feel my face heat, embarrassed. "It was nothing... really."

Issi blurts out a laugh. "I don't think you can get away with saying it was nothing. It was a success. I know the brothers were pleased with the amount of money raised." She kisses my hand. "It's going to help so many veterans, Natalie."

I nod my head, and I can't help it, but my shoulders pull back, and I stand a little taller. I am proud of all we accomplished.

Issi grimaces and turns side to side as if she's stretching out her back. "I've missed coming to Work It Out and seeing you."

I can't resist rubbing my hand across her belly. "Well, when the little one comes, you can come back. I'll sit in my office and play with the baby while you get your sweat on."

She rolls her eyes, and it's then I notice how tired she looks, not that I would ever tell her that. "That actually sounds pretty wonderful."

I nod. "Sooooo... we still don't know if you're having a boy or girl?"

Lucas groans. "No, and she's determined that it's going to be a surprise for all of us."

Issi laughs as Lucas pulls her into his arms. "It's going to be a huge surprise for us all."

I'm about to agree when I feel someone brush up against me. I know who it is before I even turn and look. "Hey," I say, way more breathlessly than I mean to.

Beau smiles down at me. "Hey, wifey. I saved you a seat."

I nod, but before I go with him, I turn to Lucas and Issi. "What about you guys? You sitting down?"

Issi shakes her head with a groan. "Those metal seats are too uncomfortable for me. I'm good standing."

I hug her one more time before waving at them as I follow Beau. He climbs the stairs to the bleachers, moving in and out of people down the aisle until we get to the top row. "Have a seat," he says, pointing at two empty places.

I look around. "Where are Ford and Lilian?"

He points down to the field. "Ford paces the whole game and can't sit. I think Lilian stays with him to keep him calm. Austin was working on an order, so I'm not sure if he'll make it, but Huddy and Elle were going to stop by."

I nod as he mentions each of his brothers. "What number is Ollie?" I ask as I look out at the field. From this distance, they all look the same.

Beau points out to the field. "He's number twelve."

I search the field until I find my nephew. "He's a goalie?"

"Yep, the coach let him play there a few weeks ago, and he did so well that they keep him there now."

I nod and watch as the teams go back and forth on the field. When Ollie blocks a goal, I stand up and cheer, screaming Ollie's name. I swear he hears me as he looks up at where we're seated, waving wildly.

When I sit down, I'm covering my mouth with my hands, excited. I turn to Beau. "Oh my God, do you think I embarrassed him? I was too loud, wasn't I?"

Beau chuckles. "No way. That kid is eating it up."

I look out on the field, and sure enough, Ollie is pointing up here with a big smile on his face. I wave at him again and then hold my hands in my lap. I take a deep breath, enjoying being outside, watching my nephew play with his friends, sitting in the stands next to Beau. We are watching the game when I see two women sitting in the aisle below us. They're both looking toward Beau and me, and I try to ignore them and focus on the game being played in front of us.

One of the women puts her hand on my knee to get my attention. "Hey," she says.

I smile, about to say hi when she leans past me. "Hey, Beau."

His hand goes to my thigh and squeezes. "Hey, Marlene. This is my wife, Natalie. Natalie, this is Marlene. Her son and Ollie have had a few playdates."

I nod with a smile fixed on my face. "Oh great, yeah, it's nice to meet you."

She nods, and her smile tightens as she looks at me before brightening up again when she looks at Beau. "So I'm thinking about the next playdate, and I think we should go to the new pizza place across town. They have the video games, and we can sit and talk while the boys play."

I tense. Did she really just ask my husband out on a date in front of me?

Beau coughs. "Uh, yeah, that would be fine. Nat and I would like that, wouldn't we?" he says, sliding closer to me.

Dumbfounded, I just stare at the woman and try to process it all. Has my husband been out with this woman before? Have I been a fool? After all this talk about the guy at the gym flirting with me, has he been with someone else?

I know women like Marlene, and when she sees that I'm now looking at her curiously, she smiles even more. "Hey, I haven't been, but are you the one that owns Work It Out?"

I nod, forcing a smile to my face. "Yes, that's me."

Marlene tilts her head to the side, lifts her glasses up on her head so I can see her eyes, and makes a big to-do of looking me up and down. Without her saying a word, I know exactly what she's thinking. It's not like I haven't dealt with it before—heck, ten years ago when I started teaching workout classes, I thought it myself. I'm a plus-size woman that teaches fitness classes. I now own a gym. I help people get in shape, and that look she's giving me is that she thinks I'm not fit for what I do.

I do my best to act like I'm not fazed by her judgment. "So you've never been? You should definitely come in. Any friend of Beau and Ollie's is welcome. Now, if you don't mind, this is the first time I've gotten to watch my nephew play, and I don't want to miss a second of it."

She rears back, gives me a smirk, and turns back toward the field. As soon as she does, I slide a few inches away from Beau, pushing his hand off my leg.

I will not cry. I will not cry.

My mind is going a thousand different directions, but I will not cry.

I force my attention to the game being played in front of me. I get completely entranced with the six-year-olds on the field. My eyes are glued to Ollie, and when he saves a goal, I jump up and cheer again. This time, Ollie's looking for me before I even stand up. I wave my fist in the air, and he does the same.

"Natalie."

I don't look at him. Beau says my name in a soft, pleading voice, but I don't look at him.

Until he tries again. "Natalie, baby."

I hold my hand up and hiss at him. "I'm not doing this here, Beau."

When the game is over, I don't wait for him. I make my way down the bleachers and don't stop until I'm next to Ford and Lilian.

Lilian sees me first and pulls me in for a hug. "Natalie, you're here!" I hug her tightly, and when she pulls back, she's holding me at arm's length, not letting me go. "I heard you cheering for Ollie. I was this close to being jealous when he was looking at the stands, but once I figured out it was you, I was okay." She says it all in a rush and then pulls me in for another hug. "I'm so glad you came."

I nod. "Me too. He did so well."

Ford pulls his shoulders back and pats his belly. "Yep, I taught him everything he knows."

We all laugh, and by now, Beau has joined us. The brothers shake hands, and I don't miss the look Ford gives Beau, gesturing to me with a smile.

I look around the small group. "Where are Huddy and Elle? I really enjoyed meeting her the other night."

Ford and Lilian look guilty before Lilian finally breaks the silence. "Uh, a spreadsheet is getting the best of them. They planned to come, but they had a report they needed to finish."

They both are trying to hold back a laugh as Beau looks like he's about to combust. He points at himself. "My spreadsheet? They're easy, there shouldn't be any problem. What spreadsheet is it?"

Before Ford can answer, Ollie runs toward us screaming. I barely have time to put my hands out before he's jumping into my arms. There's no way I'd stay upright if Beau wasn't behind me to hold me up. I'm laughing so hard as I hold him in my arms. "You were amazing, Ollie! I am so impressed by the way you blocked those goals."

We all laugh and listen as Ollie gives us a retelling of the game. He gives us the play-by-play. None of us complain, though. We may have sat through the whole game and watched every minute of it, but listening to Ollie tell it from his perspective is better than any game we could have watched. As we all listen, I can't help but notice that Beau is off to the side on the phone.

Ollie is jumping up and down in front of me. "Go eat with us. We're going to have pizza. Please, Aunt Natalie?"

I don't even look at Beau to see if it's okay because there's no way I'm telling the kid no. "I would love to go have some pizza with you."

When Beau joins us, he has a worried look on his face. He's taken all this time off, and I know his job is important. I'm not going to complain that he has to go in and fix something. "Go to the office. Huddy and Elle need your help, and we're all good here."

He looks at me curiously. "No, I told them to send me the report and I'd do it later tonight."

I shake my head, suddenly feeling like I need a breather and that maybe a little distance would do me some good. "No, really. Go fix it. Trust me, I know you, Beau Blaze, and you're not going to be any fun knowing some spreadsheet is out in the universe and the formulas are broken."

Everyone laughs around me, but Beau knows me well. "I can do it later. I think we need to talk."

I shake my head. "Anything we need to talk about, we can talk about later. I'll see you at home in a little while, but right now, I need to go. I have a date with a handsome young man to go play games and eat pizza."

"Pizza!" Ollie screams, and we all laugh again.

We're all walking to the parking lot, and Beau leans in next to me. "Natalie, it's not what you think."

The truth is I have at least ten questions for every damn scenario that's come across my mind since I met Marlene tonight, but I'm not going to bring it up now in front of everyone. Ollie is begging Ford and Lilian to let him ride with me, and I glare at Beau. "So I haven't been sitting at home wanting to be with you and your family and then find out you've been having dinner with my nephew and some woman and her kid?"

There's no hiding the hurt in my voice or on my face. It's there for anyone to see. I need to get myself together. "Like I said, we'll talk about this later. Please, just go and let me enjoy tonight."

"Natalie, wait! My mom and dad said I can ride with you."

Ollie is running toward us carrying a booster seat with him. I throw my hands up in the air. "Yes! Well, let's go, I'm starving."

I take the booster seat from him and set it up in my backseat.

Ollie is bouncing up and down on the balls of his feet. "Uncle Beau, you riding with us?"

"Yeah, I'm riding with you," he answers before looking at me. "If that's okay."

I don't have to answer. "Duh, Uncle Beau. You can ride with us, but none of that kissing stuff like Mom and Dad. It's so gross."

I can't help but laugh as I walk around to where Beau is. I drop the keys into his hand.

He's surprised. "You want me to drive?"

I nod. "Yeah, I need to DJ."

"DJ?" Beau and Ollie say at the same time.

I point at the door for Ollie and watch as he buckles himself in. "Yes, DJ. We just won a ball game. We need to play some victory tunes on the way to our victory dinner."

I shut his door, and Beau is standing at the passenger door with it open for me.

Ollie hollers from the back as I get in, "Are you going to play it loud, Aunt Nat?"

Beau is walking around to the driver's side, watching me through the front windshield. "You know it, kid."

As soon as Beau turns on the car, I find the music on my phone and blare the song through the speakers. The whole way across town, we sing along with the windows down. I pull the visor down to see Ollie in the back seat, and he smiles at me, nodding his head along to the music.

I join in, earning an even bigger smile from him.

Beau is quiet the whole trip. If he wanted to say anything, he would have to do it over the loud music. For just a moment, I let myself reflect on everything. It shouldn't be this hard. I love him, and he loves me. It shouldn't be this hard.

Chapter 19

Beau

I fucked up... again.

I know I did. It was stupid. One night after a game, Ford and Lilian asked me to take Ollie out to dinner so they could have a date night. It was nothing. Ollie and I were enjoying our meal when Marlene and Max showed up. Of course, Max and Ollie wanted to eat together, and we ate a meal. Marlene flirted, but I made sure to talk about Natalie, and absolutely nothing happened. But just thinking about it, I know where I fucked up. I should have told Natalie about it. Hell, I should have had Natalie there with me.

We pull into the parking lot, and Nat and Ollie are both out of the car before I can get around to their side. I reach for her hand and hold my breath, wondering if she's going to let me or not. When her hand fits into mine, I breathe out a sigh of relief.

"What do you want on your pizza, Ollie?"

As soon as she asks the question, I'm shaking my head because I know what the kid is going to answer. "Pineapple!"

She stops and looks down at him. "Pineapple? You want pineapple on your pizza?"

He nods. "I swear, it's really good, Aunt Nat. Try it with me." He points at me. "All of them say its gross, and they get me my own pizza, but they won't even try it."

Natalie holds her hand up for a high-five. Ollie doesn't hesitate and smacks his hand across hers. "Well, you're in luck, little nephew. I happen to love pineapple. Have you tried it with pepperoni and pineapple? That's my favorite."

He shakes his head. "No, but I love pepperoni, and I love pineapple." And then he squints his forehead. "Do you really like it, Aunt Nat, or are you just joking with me?"

Natalie laughs, and the sound goes all through me. I'm learning that I love to hear her laugh. "I promise. I love pineapple on my pizza. I never get to eat it, though, because this guy will only eat meat on his pizza."

Ollie jumps up and down excitedly. "Well, any time you want pineapple pizza, I'm your guy, Aunt Nat. I'll eat it with you."

They both walk ahead, and I listen to them laugh and joke with each other. All this time, I've kept their interactions limited, and they've missed out... because of me.

When we get inside, Ford is waving at us, and we make our way to a table in the back. The place is packed, and we squeeze between all the tables to get to our family. Ford, Lilian, Huddy, Elle, and Austin are all sitting down. "We went ahead and ordered pizzas since they were getting so busy. We got a little of everything," Ford says.

Ollie slides in to sit next to Ford. Nat slides in next, and then I follow, still holding her hand. I just don't want to let her go.

Natalie looks around the table. "Where are Lucas and Issi?"

Elle leans forward with a grimace on her face. "Issi was tired, so they went home."

Natalie nods, and we all listen as Ollie tells everyone what Nat's favorite kind of pizza is. When the server comes, we order drinks, and I make sure to order Nat a pepperoni and pineapple pizza. All this time, I had no idea that she even ate that on her pizza. She always just said whatever was fine when I asked her. I want to kick myself because now I'm wondering what else she has given up because of me.

We talk about the soccer game and Blaze Whiskey, and Elle asks Nat about the gym. It seems like no time at all has passed before they are bringing all the pizzas out. "And last but not least, I have a small pineapple pizza and a small pepperoni and pineapple pizza."

Natalie looks at me, surprised, and smiles. "Did you order that?"

I nod. "Yeah, I didn't know it was your favorite. I know now."

The look she gives me makes me want to order twenty more pizzas especially for her. I'm learning that it's the little things that she appreciates. I think she's happier right now than she was when I gave her the diamond earrings she's wearing.

I release her hand so we can eat, and I notice my brother across the table barely eating. "What's up, Austin? Where's Ally?"

He looks down at his plate. "She's on a date."

The whole table goes silent. "A date?"

He nods. "Yeah, a date."

I shake my head. "You fool."

Austin's jaw tightens, and I wait for him to say something. He looks around the table and then back at me. "Yeah, I'm a fool."

Thankfully, Ollie isn't aware of the change in the atmosphere because he asks Nat, "After you're finished, can you play games with me?"

Nat doesn't hesitate. "Absolutely."

I walk up to the stand and put money in to buy some game cards. When I get back to the table, I hand one to Ollie and one to Nat.

Nat is biting into her pizza, and Ollie is practically bouncing in the seat next to her. I'm about to offer to take him so she can eat, but she puts the pizza down and pats her stomach. "I think I've had enough. I think we should go play. What do you think, Ollie?"

I'm about to tell her she should eat when Ollie practically vibrates in his seat.

"Yes!" he cries, and I'm practically shoved out of the booth so they can go.

"You want me to come with you?" I ask Nat.

She pats me on the chest. "Nope, you go ahead and eat. We're fine."

I sit back down and try to eat. The conversation goes on around us, but I know it won't take long for any of them to ask what's on everyone's mind.

"How's it going?" Ford asks first.

And then Huddy joins in. "Yeah, did you get your shit together?"

I can't help but laugh at his bluntness, but my hands fist on the table. "Yep, we're working it all out. I won't let her leave me. I've been a fool, but I'm making it right."

I look at Austin when I say the word *fool*. He rolls his eyes and looks back down at the table.

We talk about everything but mostly about Isabella and Lucas. I'm just about to get up and go search for Nat when one of Ollie's friends runs into the dining room. "Beau, come quick, Ollie needs you."

Every one of us are out of our seats. My stomach drops, wondering what has happened, and we follow the boy through the maze of the arcade games and people until I see Ollie sitting on the floor next to Natalie.

My nephew is all right, but Natalie isn't. She's sitting huddled up with her head in her lap. Ollie looks up at me with tears in his eyes. "Uncle Beau, she just sat down like this. She said her head hurts and she can't open her eyes. Is she going to be okay?"

Fuck, she has a migraine. I should have thought about this. All the noise and the flashing lights. "You did the right thing, Ollie. Thank you for staying with her. I know you're scared, but she's going to be all right, I promise. Tell your dad and everyone that she has a migraine and I'm taking her home, okay?"

He nods, but he doesn't let go of Nat. He leans in and kisses her arm. "I love you, Aunt Nat."

She lifts her head. "I love you too, Ollie."

I put my hand on his back. "All right, I'm going to take her, okay?"

He releases his hold on her, and I pick her up in my arms. "Hold on, baby. I'm going to get you out of here."

It scares me that she doesn't answer me; she just lays her head against my chest. Ford puts his hand on my shoulder. "Call me if you need anything."

I nod my head and walk through the arcade and then through the dining room. Austin is walking with us and is holding doors open. He even digs the keys from my pocket to open the car door for us. Normally, he'd have some kind of smart-ass remark, but he doesn't say a thing. I settle Nat into the car, lay her seat all the way back, and put the seat belt on her. I shut the door as quietly as possible.

"Is she okay?" my brother asks.

"Yeah, she'll be fine. She gets migraines, and I didn't even think to warn her about the arcade. All those flashing lights and the noise in there is what set it off, I'm sure."

He follows me around the car. "Call me if you need anything."

I get in the car, start it, and turn the radio off. "I'll call you. Thanks, brother."

The drive home is quiet, and I keep looking over at Nat, who is now curled up in a ball with her arm covering her eyes.

I pull straight into the garage and then go around to help her out. Without question, I pull her into my arms. "I can walk," she mutters.

"I can carry you, too."

It's awkward getting the door open with her in my arms, but I'm not going to put her down. I get through the door and then take her straight upstairs. I set her on her feet just long enough to pull the covers back, and then I help her into bed.

I remove her shoes, then her socks, and then I peel her leggings down her body before pulling the cover over her.

I run into the bathroom and open the medicine cabinet. I knock over bottles until I find the one I need. I grab a cup and fill it up with water and make my way back to the bedroom. I set the water and bottle down on the nightstand and then lean over Natalie. "Baby, I need you to sit up and take this for me, okay?"

She moans, and I hate the sound. I know she's in pain, but the pills help her. She has to take them.

"Nat, here, baby. I'll help you."

I put my hands under her and lift her up, grabbing my pillow and putting it under her too. She sits up a little higher, clenching her eyes shut the entire time. I grab the bottle and take a pill out and then grab the water. "Take the pill. Then you can rest."

She does as I ask, and after she takes a second drink of water, I help her back down. I'm about to get up when she grabs my arm. "Beau."

"I'm just going to turn off the light, grab an ice pack for your head, and then I'm going to lie down with you, okay?"

"K," she mumbles.

I run down to the kitchen and grab the ice pack before running back upstairs.

I go to turn off the bedroom light, and then I make my way to my side of the bed in the dark. I strip down to my underwear and then climb in on my side.

I'm facing her, and once my eyes adjust, I can see her chest expand with each breath she takes. Gently, I lay the ice pack across her forehead.

"Beau."

I reach for her, putting my hand in hers and threading our fingers together. "I'm right here, baby."

"I'm so embarrassed. It's probably good you never wanted me to go out to dinner with you and your family. Poor Ollie, I bet I embarrassed him in front of his friends. It just came on so fast and so hard."

She sounds almost panicked, and I stroke her arm to try and soothe her. "Ollie wasn't embarrassed at all.

He was worried about you, but I told him he did a good job. My phone has been blowing up since I got you home. I know our family is worried about you."

She reaches out, slapping the air between us. "Call Ollie and tell him I'm fine. He was so upset."

I grab my phone off the nightstand and call Ford. He answers on the first ring. "How's Natalie?"

I speak softly into the phone. "She's fine. She's already taken her medicine, and she's in bed. She's worried about Ollie, though."

"Ollie is fine. Tell her not to worry about anything. We're all good, and she needs to get better."

I glance over at Natalie and nod my head. "I'll tell her. Thank you, brother. Talk to you tomorrow."

I put my hand on Nat's. "Ollie's fine. They're all just worried about you."

"I'm fine," she says. The medicine works quickly normally, but I lie here quietly because maybe going to sleep will help her feel better faster. I hate it when she gets like this. I would do anything to take away the pain.

Minutes have passed by before she says anything. "I don't like that Marlene."

I reach my other hand out and stroke my hand softly up and down her arm. "Is that what brought the migraine on?"

She groans. "No, we can thank all the flashing lights and the loud noise of the arcade for that."

"Shit, I'm sorry. I should have known it would trigger one, Nat. I should have gone in there with Ollie instead of you."

Her voice is soft, and she talks slowly. "Are you kidding? Ollie and I had a blast. I can handle a small migraine. It was worth it."

I grumble, "I still should have been there."

She turns toward me, but her eyes are still closed. "Beau, things are going to come up. You're going to go back to work, and we're going to do separate things. I just wasn't thinking. Maybe the next time, I should be better prepared. Maybe take my medicine with me."

"Or just not go in the arcade."

She shakes her head and groans. "No, I'm sure our kids are going to want to go in an arcade, Beau. I'll want to be part of the fun. I'm not going to want to miss anything."

As if I need any further proof that Nat is different than my mom. Of course, she would do something for our kids if it causes her pain but makes them happy. She's that kind of woman. She's completely selfless. "You're strong, Natalie. Probably the strongest woman I know. I should have known you would be selfless when it comes to our kids. I never should have doubted you."

She reaches out and puts her hand on my bare chest. She seems to test opening her eyes. At first, she just peeks through them, and when she finds there is no light in the room at all, she's able to open them a little further. "I am strong, Beau. I can handle a lot of things... but I can't handle you hanging out with Marlene."

I open my mouth to tell her what happened, but she doesn't let me. "You don't have to tell me. I'm sure I can guess; I know women like Marlene. I'm sure you were somewhere with Ollie, and she and her son showed up. I know it was all innocent, and I know you wouldn't cheat on me, but if it's okay, I would like to ask you…"

She stops and takes a breath.

"Anything. You can ask me for anything, Nat, and the answer is yes."

"I would just like for you to not spend time with her. She wants you, Beau, and I'm not willing to share."

I let out a hard, slow breath. I don't deserve her. I know I don't, but just as soon as that thought comes, I know I'll do anything to be a better man—one that does deserve her. "You don't have to worry about me with any other woman. You are and always will be the only woman for me."

She smiles and closes her eyes. "Will you hold me, Beau?"

I scoot closer to her and gently pull her into my arms. "Always."

I want to hold her tighter, but I don't dare. I force myself to hold her softly when all I want to do is kiss her until she doesn't have any doubts about me, her or us. After the way I've behaved this past year, I know she doesn't have faith in me. Hell, no one would blame her after the way that Marlena acted at Ollie's game.

"Nat?"

She doesn't answer. Her breathing has slowed, and I listen as she lets out a tiny whimper in her sleep. She scoots closer to me. "Beau?"

I kiss the top of her head. "Yeah, baby?"

Her words are slurred, and she's half asleep, but I can make out her requests. "Don't leave me, okay?"

I kiss her again. "Never."

Chapter 20

Natalie

The smell of coffee and bacon hits my nose.

I open one eye, the remnants of last night's migraine still fresh on my mind.

When there's no pain, I open both eyes and look at my husband, who is fully dressed. He points at the tray on the bed. "Breakfast... if you're up for it."

I sit up gingerly and nod my head. "I'm good as new."

He helps me up nonetheless. Once I have the pillows stacked at my back, he hands me the cup of coffee, and I take a small sip. "Mmmm, this is perfect."

He nods. "Do you feel like going to the hospital?"

I roll my eyes. "The hospital? Beau, I'm fine. I really am."

He smiles gently at me. "I know. I just thought you may want to go see your new nephew."

"New nephew..." I set the cup on the nightstand. "Beau, are you telling me that Issi and Lucas had the baby?"

He nods, his smile widening. "She was in labor all night. She had him around five this morning."

I jump out of bed. "And you're just telling me? Oh Beau, you missed it."

He takes a bite of bacon off the plate. "I wasn't going to leave you. It's fine. We can go now."

I race around the room, grabbing clothes. "You should have been there. It's your family and—"

He comes up to me. "You're my family, and I should have stayed with you to make sure you're okay. Now that you're better, you and I will go together."

I put my hand to his chest. "Give me five minutes." I go to my tiptoes and kiss him quickly. "Five minutes."

I squeal as I race out of the bedroom and into the bathroom. I turn on the shower and pull off my clothes. I wrap my hair in a knot at the top of my head, and then I'm in and out of the shower in no time. I brush my teeth, put lotion on, and then after getting dressed in shorts and a blouse, I put some mascara and lip gloss on before going out to the bedroom.

Beau is sitting on the bed. "Wow, that has to be the quickest shower ever."

"Let's go, let's go. My sandals are downstairs."

He's laughing as he follows me down the stairs. I slip on my sandals and make my way out to the garage. I get in the passenger side and impatiently tap my foot on the floorboard as I wait for Beau to come out.

Finally, he comes out of the house and gets in. "Here. You have to eat something."

He hands me a yogurt and a banana with a bottle of water. "You are too good to me."

He's smiling as he looks at the rearview mirror and is backing out of the garage. We make the drive into Jasper, and after stopping at the gift shop, we find the maternity ward.

When we stop at the nurses' station, I'm practically bouncing with excitement. "Hi, we're here to see Lucas and Isabella Blaze."

The nurse blushes from head to toe when she looks at Beau. I roll my eyes and smile up at him. He's clueless, and I'm sure he missed it because he's had his eyes on me. "What is it? What's wrong?"

"Nothing's wrong. Everything's perfect."

The nurse looks up from the computer. "Room 318. It's down the hall and around the corner."

I grab Beau's hand and take off down the hall. He's carrying flowers, and I'm carrying a stuffed animal. "Did they pick a name?"

"Lucas Jr. My brother is so original." Beau laughs.

"Aww. A boy! We can call him LJ. I love it."

We get outside of room 318 and knock softly. Lucas comes to the door, smiling ear to ear. He pulls it open and holds his hand out. "Come on in. The party's all here."

We walk across the threshold, and for the number of people in the room, it's remarkably quiet. We wave at everyone and whisper hello. Ollie comes right up to us, and I kneel at his feet. "Nat, are you okay? You scared me."

I wrap the little boy up in my arms. "I am perfect because of you. Thank you for staying with me and sending your friend to go get Beau."

He puts his little hand on my cheek. "I'm so glad you're okay."

"I'm perfect now because you were so quick to help me. Now how about you introduce me to your brand-new cousin?"

He grabs my hand, and I follow him to where Issi is in the bed, holding the cutest little baby ever. I set the stuffed animal on the windowsill, and Beau puts the flowers next to it. Walking over to the bed, I put my hand over my mouth and gasp. "Oh my God, Issi, he's precious."

Ollie is telling us all about LJ. "He cries when he's hungry and he sleeps alllll the time." He goes on and on, and I laugh softly at the way Ollie's talking about his cousin. I press my finger to the end of his nose. "Well, I'm sure when you were younger, you did the exact same thing."

Ford gets Ollie's attention, leaving Beau and me with Issi. "Issi, he's beautiful."

She lifts him up. "Do you want to hold him?"

I gasp again, putting my hand to my heart. "Are you sure? I can wait until he's bigger. I'm fine just looking at him."

Issi laughs. "Don't be ridiculous. Plus, remember you're going to be holding him while I work out. That was the deal. You might as well get some practice in now."

I can't even laugh at her joke. I take the tiny bundle in my arms, and all I can do is stare down at him. From the jostling, he's opened his eyes, and he's looking up at me. His eyes are a light blue, and I can't look away.

Choking back a sob, I tell her, "He's perfect, you guys. My goodness, he just steals your heart right out of your chest."

I don't know how much times passes by, but eventually, LJ starts to get restless. I give him back to Lucas, and he stands next to his brother. Beau is staring at me, his mouth hanging open, but he closes it when Lucas puts the baby in his arms. "All right, big bro. Your turn."

Beau doesn't hesitate. He takes his nephew in his arms and stares down at him. I can't help it. Instantly, my ovaries feel as if they are going to explode.

A baby in Beau's arms causes my whole body to heat.

He looks up from the baby and stares right at me. Issi is talking to me about something, and I should feel bad for not paying attention, but I can't look away from my husband. He sees it. There's no way he doesn't.

He clears his throat and then looks down at his nephew in his arms. "He's perfect, bub."

Lucas is looking at the baby proudly, and I turn to Issi. "I'm so sorry. I'm listening."

Issi laughs softly and reaches for my hand. "Oh, I know exactly what you were doing."

My face heats, and I can feel the people in the room looking at me, but luckily no one else seems to know just what happened.

Beau and I stay for another few minutes until the nurse comes in and runs everyone out. After hugging, we all go outside the hospital.

"We're going to get lunch at Red's. You guys want to join us?"

The question comes from Huddy, and I look up at Beau. He answers his brother without even looking at me. "No, I think we're going to head home."

We hug everyone again, and after extra hugs to Ollie, Beau and I get in the car and drive in the opposite direction. "We could have gone to eat with them if you wanted. I really am feeling fine."

Beau shrugs. "Nope, we need to go home. I'll feed you there."

My forehead creases as I gaze out the front window. Beau is acting weird, but I just lay my head back on the seat and watch the scenery go by.

He doesn't say anything else except to ask me how my head is doing.

"It's fine. I really am good."

Is that why he didn't want to go eat with his family?

When we get home, we walk into the house, and he grabs my hand. "Come with me."

I walk with him up the stairs, and as soon as we're in the bedroom, he releases his hold on me. "Go grab your birth control."

My mouth drops, and I close it back. I go into the bathroom and grab the small case and then go back in the bedroom. "It's here. I promise, I take it every day. I just forgot this morning, but I'll take it now."

Beau grabs the package from my hand. "Wait... can we talk first?"

I stare at the way he's gripping the birth control in his hand. "Uh, sure... we can talk."

He tosses the case on the nightstand. "I want you to stop taking them. Is it safe to just stop taking them or do we need to go talk to a doctor?"

My eyes round. "You want me to stop taking them?"

His jaw is pulled tight. It's almost like he's barely hanging on. "Yes. More than anything, yes."

I shake my head, unsure. "Beau..."

He cuts me off. "I saw you, baby. I saw you holding LJ. Don't lie to me... don't lie to yourself and say you're not ready."

I jut my chin at him. "I told you I was ready... it's you that I'm not sure is ready. Two weeks ago, you were doing everything you could to make sure we didn't get pregnant. Two weeks ago, I thought you never wanted kids."

He rams his hand through his hair, causing it to stick up everywhere. "Two weeks ago, I was an idiot. Seeing you with LJ in your arms... I want that. I want you to hold our baby in your arms, and I don't want to wait any longer."

"You sure about this... you want a baby?"

He comes over to me and puts his hands at my waist. "I want your baby."

I go to my tiptoes and wrap my arms around his neck. "I want that too, Beau."

Excitement fills his face, and he picks me up, swinging me around in his arms. I'm laughing until he stops swinging and lets me slide down his body. As soon as my feet hit the floor, I'm tugging at his shirt. "We should start now."

He lifts his arms above his head. "I agree."

As soon as his shirt is off, my lips are on his chest. Between kisses, I tell him, "Seeing you with LJ had the same effect on me, Beau. You look good holding a baby."

He lifts me up and tosses me onto the bed before pulling at my shorts. "I need you, Nat."

I reach down between us and wrap my hand around his girth. I try to stroke him through the material of his pants, and he grunts as I tug on him. "Yes, you do," I tell him.

He leans down to kiss me. "I'm going to put a baby in you, Nat."

I laugh because I know it doesn't happen like that. It will take a while to conceive, but I'm more than willing to start now. "Yes."

We make love, and I feel ready for whatever life throws at us because we can handle anything... as long as we're together.

Epilogue

Beau

I can't stop smiling.

It's so bad that even during the weekly meeting that I'm sitting in, my brothers just keep looking at me and shaking their heads. After they've each taken their turns, I finally ask the question. "What? What are you all shaking your heads about?"

Huddy leans forward. "I'm just happy for you, man. It's about time is all."

Ford smirks. "Yeah, it's nice seeing you smiling."

Austin slaps his hand on the table and then waves it up and down at me. "This is definitely better than when you were smiling about all those fuckin' spreadsheets you were pushing on us."

I hold the papers up in my hand. "Well, don't you worry. I still have spreadsheets, I'm just waiting my turn."

I try to get the topic of conversation off me. "Anyone heard from Lucas? How are LJ and Issi doing?"

It's been a few weeks since LJ was born, and Lucas is still working from home. Ford leans back in his chair, fiddling a pen between his fingers. "Lilian, Ollie, and I went to see them last night. They're all doing well."

I clasp my hands together on the table in front of me. I can't help but smile as I look around at my brothers. We went through a lot growing up, and I never would have imagined that we would be where we are right now. Our company is thriving. Our brother is back from the military, everyone is getting married and talking about kids. Well, everyone but Austin. I look over at him, and he's looking down at the paper in front of him with a grim look on his face.

"Austin?"

He lifts his head, and instantly there's a smile on his face. It's not a real one; it's the one he uses when he's trying to make the world think he's okay. In most cases, no one knows, but I can tell something is off with him. He starts to speak, and it's a stutter before he gets his words formed. "Yeah, my turn? The distillery is going great. Online orders are up this month, and we've been super busy. I may have to hire a few more hands soon, but it's a good problem to have."

I wait for him to continue. I wait for some joke or some off the wall inappropriate comment, but it never comes. He's staring back at me, and the more I look at him, the more his fake smile drops from his face.

Ford clears his throat, and it's obvious that he knows something's up too. If it was any of us other brothers, we'd call them out on it, but you can't do that with Austin. Nope; with him, you have to wait until you're one on one. Otherwise, all you get is some kind of wisecrack from him.

Ford nods at me, basically letting me know that I'm up on dealing with Austin. He continues the meeting. I take my turn and go over the quarters revenue, profits, and margins. By the end of my time, everyone is basically yawning and ready to run out of here. When everyone is walking out, I ask Austin to hang back.

"What's up, big brother?"

I point to the seat next to me, and he laughs. "Oh, is it that kind of talk? What am I in trouble for?"

I shake my head. "You're not in trouble. I just want to talk to you."

He falls down in the chair and leans on the table, his arms spread out. "Okay, talk."

I lean back in my chair, debating on where to go with this. I know my brother, and if I say the wrong thing, he'll clam up on me. "What's going on with you?"

He scratches his chin. "Uh, nothing's going on with me."

"Bullshit."

Austin's face turns red, and he looks away from me. He was always the worst liar. "Nothing's going on with me. I'm good."

I cross my arms over my chest. "Where's Ally been? She still dating that guy?"

He crosses his arms over his chest. "They broke up."

I nod my head. "Well, that's good, right?"

He nods, but his face is grim. "You're not going to let me out of here until I talk to you, are you?"

I push my chair away from the table and block his path to the door. "Nope."

He tilts his head and looks at me and then the door. "You know I could take you, right? If nothing else, on speed alone."

I lean back, unfazed. "I'll have you know I've been working out with Natalie. I'm stronger than you think. Plus, Huddy's in the building. He's probably out there blocking the door as we speak."

Austin rolls his eyes at my antics, telling me that there really is something going on. Otherwise, he'd be running from here just to prove he could. "Look, just talk to me. I know there's something going on with you. You can't always keep things bottled up or hide behind a joke. I'm your big brother. Talk to me."

He finally nods and blows out a breath. It's like I can the see the relief on his face as he starts to talk. "Okay, fine. I'm going to marry Ally. She hasn't agreed yet, but that's my plan."

I clap my hands together, excited. It's no secret that Ally and Austin are meant to be together. They've been best friends for what seems like forever. We always thought they'd end up together. "What? That's great, Austin."

He holds his hand up. "And we're going to have a baby. She's pregnant."

I can't help it. If maybe I'd had some warning, I wouldn't react so badly, but it all is happening so fast. I'm shaking my head, stumped. "Pregnant? But you can't—"

He cuts me off with a look. I don't get to finish the sentence, but he knows exactly what I was going to say. Austin can't father a child. There was an accident when he was younger, and the doctors told him that he would be unable to have children. My thoughts run rampant at what this all means, but before I can ask any more questions, Austin rolls himself toward me until he's only a foot away. He doesn't look happy; if anything, he looks intimidating. "I'm marrying Ally, and we're having a child. He or she will be my child in every way that counts." He takes a deep breath and continues, "I need you to have my back on this, Beau. I don't want to hear a list of pros and cons, or to ask me if I'm doing the right thing. You know how I feel about Ally. I'm doing this."

Searching my brother's brown eyes, I know exactly how important all this is to him. I know how he feels about Ally, even though he's tried to hide it all this time. I stand up, pulling him with me. I pull him in for a fierce hug, and when I pull back, I have my hand wrapped around the base of his neck. "You know that no matter what you do, I have your back. I just want you to be happy. That's all that matters to any of us."

He nods and pats me on the shoulder. "I'm getting there. I can't lose her, Beau. I just can't."

I pull him in for another hug. "Trust me, I understand that totally. I'm here for you. We all are, and if Ally needs anything, we got you."

He slaps me on the chest as he pulls out of my arms. "Thanks, brother." He inhales sharply. "Okay, enough of this mushy bullshit. Let's get to work."

He walks out of the conference room, and I instantly pick up my phone to call Nat. Since I got over my bullshit, I always want to talk to her. She's my person. She answers on the third ring, breathless. "Hey, you!"

I stand up and go to the window to look out at the Blaze distillery on the hill. "Hey, you're out of breath."

"I just finished a class. What's wrong?"

I shake my head. "Nothing's wrong. I just wanted to hear your voice."

I can hear the smile in her voice. "Awww, I have to tell you, I do love this side of you, Beau Blaze."

I grip the phone tighter and grunt. "Well, I love every side of you. You have time for me to come see you?"

I hear a door shutting and her chair squeak as she sits down in her chair. "You know I always have time for you."

"See you in a few minutes."

I hang up the phone to go see my wife. She's my calm. She's the person that I want to be with always, and ever since I went from thinking "I'm going to lose her" to "How am I going to keep her?" my life has changed. I believe that waking up every day to love my wife and to show her how much I love her has completely altered my life. I've let my guard down, and the difference in my life has been amazing. I love my wife... and she will forever be mine.

Want to read Austin and Ally's story? Get Always Yours here.

Also by Hope Ford

Want more of Whiskey Run?

Whiskey Run

Faithful - He's the hot, say-it-like-it-is cowboy, and he won't stop until he gets the woman he wants.

Captivated - She's a beautiful woman on the run… and I'm going to be the one to keep her.

Obsessed - She's loved him since high school and now he's back.

Seduced - He's a football player that falls in love with the small town girl.

Devoted - She's a plus size model and he's a small town mechanic.

Whiskey Run: Savage Ink

Virile - He won't let her go until he puts his mark on her.

Torrid - He'll do anything to give her what she wants.

Rigid - If you love reading about emotionally wounded men and the women that help them overcome their past, then you'll love Dawson and Emily's story.

Whiskey Run: Cowboys Love Curves

Obsessed Cowboy - She's the preacher's daughter and she's off limits.

Whiskey Run: Heroes

Ransom - He's on a mission he can't lose.

Redeem - He's in love with his sister's best friend.

Submit - She's his fake wife but he wants to make it real.

Forbid - They have a secret romance but he's about to stake his claim.

Whiskey Run: Sugar

One Night Love - Her one night stand wants more.

Rebound Love - She's falling for the rebound guy.

Second Chance Love - He is not a man to ignore... especially when he asks for a second chance.

Bad Boy Love - He's a bad boy that wants her good.

Whiskey Run: Guardians MC

Protective Biker - She needs his protection and he'll give it to her. But he's going to need her heart in exchange.

Broken Biker - There's only one woman for him...

Relentless Biker - He won't stop until he has her back.

Whiskey Men

Reluctant Husband - If you love reading about curvy women getting the hot guy, opposites attract, jealousy trope, marriage of convenience, and small-town romance, then you'll love Lucas and Isabella's story.

Something Real - If you love reading billionaire, single father, age gap, boss/employee, and small-town romance, then you'll love Ford and Lilian's story.

Coming Home - If you love reading billionaire, ex-military, age gap, forced proximity, and small-town romance, then you'll love Hudson and Elle's story.

Forever Mine - If you love reading billionaire, age gap, second chance, and small-town romance, then you'll love Beau and Natalie's story.

Always Yours - If you love reading billionaire, friends to lovers, pregnancy, and small town romance, then you'll love Austin and Ally's story.

JOIN ME!

JOIN MY NEWSLETTER

www.AuthorHopeFord.com/Subscribe

Be a Hottie!

JOIN HOPE'S HOTTIES ON FACEBOOK

www.FB.com/groups/hopeford

A place to talk about Hope Ford's books! Find out about new releases, giveaways, get exclusive content, see covers before anyone else and more!

About the Author

USA Today Bestselling Author Hope Ford writes short, steamy, sweet romances. She loves tattooed, alpha men, instant love stories, and ALWAYS happily ever afters. She has over 100 books and they are all available on Amazon.

To find me on Pinterest, Instagram, Facebook, Goodreads, and more:

www.AuthorHopeFord.com/follow-me

Want FREE BOOKS?
Go to www.authorhopeford.com/freebies

www.ingramcontent.com/pod-product-compliance
Lightning Source LLC
Chambersburg PA
CBHW020107310726
48970CB00002B/511